# Demonic Summoning for the Modern Gardener

## Gardener

*Rifton Chronicles: Book 2*

By Robinne Weiss

Published by Sandfly Books

ISBN: 978-1-0670175-2-1 (print)
ISBN: 978-1-0670175-3-8 (ebook)

Cover Design by Jenn Rackham.

Discover Robinne's other books and stories at
https://robinneweiss.com.

# Chapter 1

## *Happy Birthday*

What the hell was Aunt Rachael thinking? Katie Cochrane gazed up at the Rifton Pub. The two-storey weatherboard-clad building bore the signs of fire—black streaks of soot rose from the upper-storey windows like eyelashes. The left-hand side of the roof was buckled.

The building hadn't been much of a sight before the fire, either, based on the dingy, peeling paint, rotting windowsills, and faded sign. The place was ancient and decrepit.

"Thanks Rachael. Just what I always wanted for my thirtieth birthday—an old, burnt-out pub," she muttered. Still, she may as well have a look at the place, now that she was here. Katie unlocked the gate of the construction fence that had been erected around the building. The engineer said it was 'mostly safe' to enter—the fire had largely been confined to two of the rooms upstairs, and the building was still structurally sound ... or as sound as a structure built in 1890 could be.

Katie frowned up at the cracked weatherboards and broken windows. It might have been better if the whole thing had burnt down.

She opened the door and stepped into the dim bar area, wrinkling her nose against the biting tang of charred wood.

Through a forest of chair legs upturned on the tables, the tap handles glittered in a beam of sunlight slanting through a window. It almost looked like nothing had happened here. Katie wove between tables, running her fingers lightly over their surfaces. Gritty dust came away, turning her skin grey. How long did Rachael say the pub had been abandoned? The bar was wood, worn and polished to softness. Baby corrugate wrapped around the base—a classic Kiwi look.

The alcohol was gone, but tableware, glassware and cutlery remained in place, all of it in desperate need of a wash. She opened the fridge behind the bar. The reek of death and dirty socks assaulted her. *Gah!* She slammed the door shut again. It would take a lot of bleach to make that thing useable again.

It wasn't until she reached the kitchen that Katie began to consider actually keeping the pub. Four commercial ovens and two six-burner hobs would mean she could make her own baked goods, as well as offer meals. The walk-in refrigerator and freezer (that someone had thankfully left open) looked relatively new. Racks filled with pots and pans, bakeware and utensils would meet most of her needs. She imagined the long stainless-steel bench gleaming underneath racks of cooling muffins. Maybe Aunt Rachael hadn't been so crazy after all.

Unfortunately, the kitchen and dining area were the best parts of the building. The toilets were dank and ugly—black mildew crept up walls tiled in institutional green. A handful of tiles had cracked and fallen off the walls. The men's room reeked of urine.

A narrow, carpeted staircase led upstairs to the hotel rooms. Until the 1960s, pubs were required to offer at least six rooms of accommodation, and even after the requirement was lifted, there were heavy fines if a pub didn't have accommodation. Those fines were only lifted in the late

1980s, so most old pubs still had rooms. This pub had been built to the letter of the law, with exactly six small rooms upstairs, which probably hadn't been renovated since the 1960s. Katie doubted they'd been rented out much in the past forty years.

At the top of the stairs, Katie poked her head into a communal bathroom across the hallway from the staircase. Of course, in a place this old, the hotel rooms wouldn't have ensuites. Its fixtures were dated, but it was clean. Then she turned to her right, away from the burnt end of the hallway. Room One looked like a staff break room, with a kettle, a microwave, a couple of ashtrays, a small television, and some beat-up couches and chairs. The smell of stale cigarettes overpowered the charred wood smell that pervaded the upper floor, and made Katie wrinkle her nose.

Room Two had obviously been used as an office. An old steel desk was flanked by two tall filing cabinets. Katie rifled through the drawers and found accounts and ledgers going back to the early 1900s. Who saved that stuff for over a hundred years? Across the hallway, Rooms Five and Six were outfitted with beds and bedside tables, but both rooms were cluttered with cardboard boxes of old dishware, stained table linens, ancient appliances, and who knew what else.

The floor of the hallway outside Rooms Three and Four was blackened—the carpet charred and brittle underfoot. Katie stepped gingerly, thinking the engineer's 'mostly safe' could involve a burnt floorboard giving way underfoot if she was unlucky.

Both rooms' doors were charred and splintered. Katie peeked into Room Three first. The damage wasn't as bad as she expected. The fire must have entered through the door, and the heavy charring ended about halfway to the window. None of the furniture in the room would be salvageable, but who would have wanted cheap 1950s bedside tables or a battered, dark veneered chest of drawers anyway, fire or no fire?

Room Four was a wreck. The bed was blackened, veneer pulling away from the wood in curling layers. The edges of the duvet were burnt into ragged scallops, and the pillow resembled an over-toasted marshmallow. The chest of drawers, once painted white, was streaked with black, the paint flaking off in crumbly charcoal scales. Katie's eyes followed the scorch marks up the wall to the ceiling. *Damn!* The entire ceiling was black, and sunlight shone through a circular hole burned straight through to the roof. She frowned at the hole. How would a fire make such a perfect circle? Dropping her gaze to the floor directly under the hole, she noted a corresponding blackened circle on the floor. What perfectly circular object sat there and burned, with no bits left behind?

Of course, the investigators must have taken whatever it was away—there was no question that whatever sat here had been the source of the fire. It looked like they'd marked it— someone had drawn a chalk circle around the blackened area on the floor.

Outside of the burnt circle, the wooden floor was in relatively good shape. It was filthy, but solid, with minimal burning. Katie scuffed her shoe in a pile of what looked like soil and shook her head. What the hell had happened in this room? Meth lab? She'd been assured there were no traces of drugs in the building. Maybe she could ask the realtor if they had more information about the fire.

Back on the ground floor, Katie pulled out a bar stool, wiped it clean, and sat down with her phone to text Aunt Rachael.

**I just had a look at the birthday gift
you bought for me. You have a LOT
of explaining to do!**

A smiling emoji popped up, followed by the words,
**You're welcome! I can't wait to
see what you do with it!**

Katie laughed. Of course, Aunt Rachael assumed Katie
would renovate and start her own business, rather than run
screaming from the ageing mess of a building.

She closed her eyes and imagined the bar top gleaming,
one of her staff mopping up a puddle of beer with a cloth. She
heard the clink of glasses, the rattle of pans in the kitchen, the
sizzle of a basket of chips being lowered into the fryer. She
smelled the yeast and cinnamon of the morning baking, the
bite of strong coffee, the rich savoury aromas of garlic and
mushrooms in her signature pies.

When she opened her eyes, the vision shattered against the
reality of an ancient building—dark, musty, and half-
destroyed by fire.

Aunt Rachael was crazy.

# Chapter 2

## *A Cup of Inspiration*

The following day, Katie met up with her friend Tui for a coffee.

"She gave you a *pub*? Oh my god. That's awesome!" Tui squealed and then lowered her voice. "Does that mean you're quitting? Please, tell me you're quitting that shitty job."

Katie sighed. "It's not the job, it's the boss that's shitty."

"Truth. But you should still quit." Tui took a sip of her latte.

"The building is half burnt down, it's over a hundred and thirty years old, and it's disgusting. Not to mention it's out in the little town of Rifton, not even here in Christchurch."

Tui shrugged. "So, you renovate. And you make it so good, people will drive out from the city to eat there."

"Do you know how much renovating that place would cost?" The prospect terrified Katie. Where would she get the money?

"No, and I bet you don't know either. Come on, Katie, at least explore the option. I can help."

"I've already decided to sell it. The realtor said there were two other buyers interested when Aunt Rachael bought it—he's willing to contact them and see if they're still keen."

"Did he say what it's worth?"

Katie grimaced. "Not much." Not nearly enough to buy a nice place and start her own restaurant. But maybe enough to quit her job and spend some time looking for a different one.

"Katie, you've always said your dream is to open your own restaurant. Why would you throw this opportunity away?"

"You haven't seen this place. It's a pit. Aunt Rachael wasn't thinking when she bought it."

Tui huffed. "I still think it's worth at least *considering* the idea. Have it inspected, get a few quotes for renovations. It's not every day someone gifts you a pub."

Yes, owning a restaurant was Katie's dream, but the state of the Rifton Pub was so far from her dream, it wasn't going to happen. "It's not the right building. I can sell it and put the money towards a place that will actually work for me—one that maybe doesn't have a great gaping hole in the roof." It was the sensible thing to do. The safe thing to do.

Katie checked the time. "Shit. I've got to get to work. It was so good to see you. I feel like I never get to socialise at all these days." Katie swigged the last of her coffee and stood.

Tui shrugged her coat on. "When's your next day off? We'll go do something fun together."

"That'd be great. I'll let you know when next week's staffing schedule is posted." Katie hurried out to her car and headed to work.

Katie lifted the perfectly seared salmon filet out of the frying pan and placed it onto a wire rack. While the salmon rested, she arranged two perfect leaves of buttercrunch lettuce on a plate, and then pulled out the vegetable pickles she'd made earlier. It had been a scramble to come up with an alternative side when she discovered they were out of the usual broccolini. It wasn't the first time the head chef had stuffed up on ordering. But she was pleased with the quick pickles she'd made—thin medallions of deep pink beets, bright orange carrots, and cream-coloured ginger; delicate rings of onion; and crunchy green beans. She placed each vegetable on the plate individually, arranging the colours and shapes into a pleasing array beside the lettuce. Then she carefully placed the salmon on the bed of lettuce and topped it with a tiny sprig of microgreen basil. She smiled at her handiwork. The colours of the vegetables made the whole dish pop—it looked so much better than limp broccolini. Not that she didn't love broccolini, but this looked fresh and exciting by comparison.

She was lifting the plate to place it on the serving window when Dante, the head chef, stormed through the kitchen. "What the hell is that?"

He wasn't supposed to be here tonight. Katie's grip involuntarily tightened on the plate. "It's salmon."

"What the fuck have you done to it?" He flicked at the pickles with a finger, disturbing their artful placement. "Where's the broccolini?"

"There *was* no broccolini, so I improvised with the vegetables we had on hand."

"What do you mean, there was no broccolini? Did you even look?"

Katie resisted the urge to throw the plate at him. "I did. And Bella double-checked for me."

Dante cursed. "Bloody useless staff here. Can't even open their eyes." He stormed into the walk-in refrigerator. Katie rearranged the pickles and set the plate on the serving window.

"Who the fuck used all the broccolini?" Dante roared, returning from his search. "And what makes you think you can just make up shit like ... pickles ... and send it out there. Is this some sort of Asian food? This is a French restaurant. Our customers expect broccolini."

Yeah, because broccolini, bred in Japan, was so French, and had Dante never heard of vegetables à la Grecque? Did he think because Katie's grandma was Chinese, she couldn't cook French food? Katie bit back the temptation to tell Dante to fuck off. "Actually, the servers are all telling folks the salmon comes with vegetable pickles tonight." Dante was right about one thing—customers expected what was on the menu, and Katie knew better than to surprise them with a substitution.

"And what do we do when we run out of beets and carrots for our other dishes?"

"I've already added beets, carrots *and* broccolini to the list for this week's vegetable order." And had Dante not come in unexpectedly on his night off, the vegetables would have been ordered and delivered before he ever knew about it. Not that it was Katie's job to do it, but if Dante couldn't remember to order broccolini, *someone* had to.

Tony backed into the kitchen, pushing the door open with his butt as he balanced a large tray of dirty dishes in his hands. "Katie, those pickles are a hit!" He turned and blanched when his eyes met Dante's scowl. He quickly scuttled through to the dishwasher, dishes rattling as if in fear.

Mel called in through the window. "Katie, someone's asking if they can get those pickles as a separate side?"

Dante's scowl deepened and he pushed into Katie's personal space, looming over her. "You don't make substitutions in *my* kitchen."

With a supreme effort, Katie held her ground and kept her voice light. "I'm your sous chef. That means when you're not here, it's *my* kitchen. Anyway, why are you here? Aren't you supposed to be off tonight?"

Dante's eyes flashed pure hatred. The muscles of his jaw

flexed and his hands were balled at his sides. Would he hit her? It wasn't the first time Katie had wondered that. She refused to back down.

"It's none of your fucking business what I'm doing here." Dante stormed to the office, and a moment later, strode back out. He barged through the kitchen, scowling at all the staff, and then burst through the back door, slamming it behind him.

Katie blew out a breath, pressing her hands to her stomach to calm the jitters. The kitchen staff were frozen, everyone staring at her in dead silence. She turned to the window, where Mel still waited, eyes wide. "Yes, I can do the pickles as a side." Then she addressed the rest of the kitchen in a voice she hoped didn't reveal how shaky she felt. "Back to work everyone. There are customers waiting for their orders."

She tried to lose herself in the rhythm of the kitchen. Cooking was her happy place. Creating beautiful and delicious meals that gave people joy was a rush like no other. And with her hastily invented pickles flying out of the kitchen all night, she forgot all about Dante and his overbearing, superior attitude.

When she finally stepped out the door to go home, she was exhausted, but calm and centred. Her culinary instincts had been validated tonight. The customers appreciated her, even if her boss didn't.

Her good mood shattered when she arrived at her car. All four tyres were flat. She swore.

Tony, his car parked next to hers, approached. "What's wrong?" He rounded his car. "Damn."

Katie stood frozen, her heart sinking. How the hell do you end up with *four* flat tyres? Only by having them slashed.

Tony walked slowly around Katie's car, then bent to pick something up.

"That's a kitchen knife," Katie said. "One of ours."

Tony nodded. "Jill was looking for it this evening."

"But who—" Katie's stomach clenched.

"Dante," they said in unison.

Tony drove Katie home. She held herself together until she'd closed her apartment door behind her. Then she burst into angry tears and threw herself onto the couch. She had done nothing wrong this evening. She'd done exactly what Dante would have in the same situation. Except she was certain her pickles were better than anything Dante would have come up with—she was way more creative than he was. Did he feel threatened by her? Maybe that's why he was such a dick to her.

It still didn't justify slashing her tyres. Or shouting at her in the kitchen. Or all the other verbal abuse she had put up with from him in the past.

*You could quit.* The tantalising thought hovered in her mind.

And feel like a failure? Give in to Dante's vitriol like a coward? That's exactly what the man wanted.

*Fuck Dante. You have an opportunity to show Dante and the world what an awesome chef you are.*

The Rifton Pub. But she'd already asked the realtor to re-sell it.

*It's not sold yet.*

Unfortunately, the place was a wreck. The prospect of turning it into the restaurant she dreamed of was daunting.

*What, are you afraid of hard work? Do you really want to spend your career being beaten down by arseholes like Dante instead of owning your own restaurant? The best thing you can do to piss off Dante is to successfully run your own place.*

Katie sat up. She wiped the tears from her eyes. She could run a kitchen where staff like Dante weren't welcome. The thought of firing Dante brought a smile to her face. Not that she'd ever hire him in the first place, but it might almost be worth it, just to be able to fire him.

If she had her own kitchen, she could make all the pickles she wanted. She could experiment with the flavours she loved. She could substitute any damn thing she liked on the menu.

She snatched up her phone. It was nearly midnight. The realtor wouldn't be there, but she'd leave a message on his answering machine.

After leaving her message, she texted Tui. The woman was a night owl, and Katie had no doubt she was still awake.

**I've decided to keep the pub.**

Tui's response came almost immediately.

**Yasss! You go girl!**

**Meet me there tomorrow morning?**

**Sure thing. Don't expect me before 10, though.**

Katie had come prepared, armed with cleaning rags and towels, rubber gloves, a bucket, mop, and broom, and a new box of rubbish bags. It might be easier to envision the pub makeover if it was at least clean.

First order of business was to turn the power back on. Someone had wisely thrown the main switch after the fire. Katie hadn't touched the power on her first visit, though the realtor had assured her it was safe to do so. Now she squinted at the fuse box in the dank hallway outside the toilets. The sight was not reassuring—visible wires connected to chunky ceramic fuses in an open-fronted wooden box that looked like it had been banged together by a ten-year-old. It was nothing like the tidy modern electrical switchboards in the restaurants she'd worked in. How could this possibly be safe? When was the electrical system in the building last updated?

Bracing for an explosion or sparks, Katie flipped the main power switch. Nothing happened. She let out her breath and searched for the light switch. It was one of those old black Bakelite numbers—she definitely needed to have an electrician out. She flipped it on, and the long fluorescent lights on the ceiling flickered and stuttered to life. The combination of the flickering light and the institutional green paint on the walls of the hallway would have made the perfect set for a slasher movie. *Lovely*. She flicked the light back off.

Cleaning. She would focus on cleaning and not stress about the old electrical system, burnt-out upper storey, or the pub's eerie resemblance to a crime scene.

A list would help—once thoughts were on paper, she could let them go, knowing she wouldn't forget them. Katie had bought a brand-new notebook—A5, spiral bound, 100 pages of space for to-do lists, wish lists, plans and dreams. She cleared the chairs off one of the tables, upending them on the floor. Then she sprayed the table and chairs with disinfectant and wiped them all down before taking a seat. She opened her notebook and wrote: *ring electrician—inspect whole building, get quote on new light fixtures.*

Katie turned on all the lights on the main floor in an effort to dispel the dingy gloom of the place. It didn't help much, but it was a start. She was tempted to light the wood burner—it was freezing inside, and a pile of wood and kindling still sat next to it—but she didn't know if it was safe. Had the chimney been damaged in the fire? Until she had a full report from a building inspector, she didn't want to risk it.

Cleaning would warm her up. The dining area was probably the easiest place to start—floor, tables and chairs—so she set to work.

She made two passes over the floor with her broom, wishing she had a dust mop for the second. In addition to a thick layer of dust, there were muddy footprints from the front door to the stairs, presumably left by the firefighters. Mouse droppings along the walls sent Katie back to her list to write: *ring exterminator.*

A utility closet near the toilets offered a deep sink for filling her bucket. She turned the tap. The pipe groaned and hissed, then spat out brown liquid flecked with rust flakes. She'd need a plumber, too.

After a minute, the water ran clear. There was no hot water—it would take hours before the water cylinder got up to temperature. Katie added extra soap to try to make up for the cold water.

She had just finished mopping the dining room floor when Tui appeared at the door. Katie pulled off her gloves and waved her inside.

Tui took in the dining room, floor still wet and glistening. "It's not so bad."

Katie laughed. "This is the best part. And I've just spent two hours cleaning."

Katie took Tui on a tour. Upstairs, Tui whistled. "Damn. I see why you were sceptical. It's a shithole up here." In one of the unburnt rooms, Tui flipped open a cardboard box and gasped. "Did you see these, Katie?"

Katie had peeked into one or two boxes up here, but there were dozens. She had no idea what most held. Tui lifted out a teacup and matching saucer, her face lit up as though she'd just won the lottery. The cup was dainty, with a ruffled rim and painted all over in pink roses. It was gloriously garish.

14

Katie stepped over to admire it. Peeking into the box, her jaw dropped. It was packed tight with teacups and saucers. "Is every one different?"

They both began lifting out cup after cup, unwrapping them from fifty-year-old newspaper that disintegrated as they touched it. It was a bit of a game, matching cups and saucers, because they were nearly all unique. There were flowers in every colour of the rainbow, vines snaking over handles and rims, bright geometric art deco designs, pastoral scenes, vegetables, birds, and butterflies. Some cups were all curves and frills, others were cone-shaped with wedges for handles. A few even sat upon little feet.

And when they'd emptied that box, they found seven more boxes stuffed with cups, and six boxes containing equally garish porcelain teapots matching some of the cups.

Katie stared in awe at the treasure now spread across the floor. "I reckon there's over two hundred cups."

"And I counted thirty-nine teapots," Tui said. "Some of these cups are dated. One was from 1895! Do you think they're worth anything?"

"Who cares? I'm not selling these." An idea was forming in Katie's mind. A theme for her restaurant. She imagined quirky, mismatched place settings and these gloriously ridiculous teacups in which she'd serve vegetable pickles, specialty ice creams, crème brûlée, and maybe even tea. And those teapots could serve as water pitchers on every table.

"What will you do with them?" Tui asked.

"Come downstairs and I'll tell you. I brought snacks and tea."

# Chapter 3

*The Neighbourhood's Business*

A week later, Katie and Tui were back at the Rifton Pub. Last week, they'd cleaned and cleared the ground floor. Today they were tackling the upstairs. Katie had a skip dropped off right outside the building and rented a shipping container to hold all the things she wanted to keep. By the end of the day, she wanted the place empty and clean so she could see what she had to work with for the renovations. She was pretty sure what she wanted, and she had three different contractors scheduled to visit and provide quotes in the following week.

They spent the first two hours hauling rubbish to the skip. In addition to the burnt and smoke-blackened furniture in Rooms Three and Four, there were mouldy mattresses and pillows, wobbly chairs, chests of drawers that had delaminated, electrical appliances with damaged cords, ashtrays, and threadbare towels.

"Do you think there was ever anything of value in this place?" Tui asked, wiping her hands on her jeans after they heaved the last of the bed frames into the skip.

"If there was, the previous owner already salvaged it." Katie lobbed a rubbish bag in on top of the bed.

They turned to head back inside. "What next?" Tui asked.

"I think that's about it. I'm going to sweep the floor

upstairs and call it good enough. At least now I can see what I have to work with. Thanks so much for your help."

"No worries. I'm gonna head off then, if you don't need me," Tui said with a wave. "I need a shower before work."

Katie picked up the broom after Tui left. She supposed she could have left the dirt on the floor—the contractors would be making a mess soon enough—but she had a strong urge to get the place clean. Decades of dirt had built up under the carpet she and Tui had rolled up, and she couldn't leave it there.

Dust billowed in front of her broom, and she swore the floor looked two shades lighter after she cleared the filth. She worked her way from room to room, and her dustpan filled with dirt, mouse droppings, and a few leaves and twigs.

Room Four was surprisingly clean, in spite of the ash and bits of charred wood on the floor—it was the only room that hadn't been carpeted. Why was it different from the other rooms?

A pair of dark little balls rolled across the floor as she swept out a corner. She swept them back into her pile. A few more skittered away from her as she swept the rest of the room. Curious, she crouched down and picked one up. It was steel grey, about the size of a large pea. It was segmented, and looked exactly like the little slaters she and her friend Maya used to find in the sandpit at primary school, though this one seemed to be dead.

Slaters. Great. Didn't they inhabit damp places? Hopefully once that hole in the roof was fixed, it would deal with the dampness indoors. She dropped the hapless bug into her pile of dirt and finished sweeping.

She brushed the last of the dirt into her dustpan, and then realised she'd already tied up the final rubbish bag. She frowned at the contents of the pan. It was all just dirt. She'd tip it out under the shrubbery at the back of the car park. It was a good excuse to get outdoors—escape the dust and the pervasive smell of charred wood.

Grabbing her water bottle on the way out, she headed down the stairs and into the crisp air of a sunny winter's day. She emptied her dustpan, then took a swig of water. Her arm shook as she raised the bottle. Had she ever done as much lifting as she'd done today? She'd be lucky if she could move tomorrow.

"Hello!" A short, stout woman with curly white hair waved from the footpath, then crossed the car park towards Katie. She held out her hand. "You must be the new pub owner. I'm Ellen Wright."

Katie tried not to think of how she must look, covered in dust and probably reeking of sweat. She smiled and wiped her hand on her jeans before grasping Ellen's hand. "I'm Katie. Nice to meet you. I assume you live in Rifton?"

Ellen nodded. "Been here forty-three years. That almost makes me a local." She glanced at the pub. "You've got your work cut out for you there. I wasn't sure anyone would buy the place."

Katie laughed. "Well it wouldn't have been my first choice, but my aunt thought I needed it. She bought it for me for my birthday."

Ellen's eyebrows rose. "That's a hell of a birthday gift. Are you still speaking to her?"

Katie liked this woman. "For now. We'll see how the renovations go. I'll be meeting with contractors this week. I've been clearing the place out, sorting through everything that was left behind."

Ellen's attention was caught by three women passing on the footpath. "Margaret! Pauline! Sharon!" She waved them over.

"Have you met our new publican yet?" she asked as they approached.

Katie raised a hand, a bit intimidated by these four older women. Why did they have to stop by when Katie was covered in dirt and sweat? A great impression she was making. She sighed inwardly. No doubt these old timers wouldn't like her anyway. They probably wanted to see the pub returned to its previous state, selling cheap beer and greasy chips and blaring the rugby game on a big screen. It wasn't what Katie planned. She put on a brave face and said, "Hi. I'm Katie."

Ellen introduced the others. Margaret was taller than Ellen, with a short bob of grey hair and a round face. Sharon looked like she'd spent a lifetime in the sun. The skin on her wiry frame was tanned like leather, but her eyes were bright and sharp. Pauline was by far the most striking of the group. She was tall—an Amazon compared to Katie. Her silvered hair was pulled back in a long heavy braid over which she'd tied a purple bandanna. Her jeans were faded, with holes in the knees, and she wore tall, mud-encrusted gumboots. Every one of the women exuded confidence—they were on their home turf here in this little rural township. Katie was certain she stood out to them like a turd in a fruit bowl.

She braced for the inevitable question, *Where are you from?* But the question didn't come. Instead, Margaret said, "Please tell me you're going to do breakfasts."

"And proper tea—none of that teabag shit," said Ellen.

"Well, if we're placing orders, I'd like a good carrot cake without too much frosting," added Sharon.

Pauline flapped a hand at the other women. "Give the poor girl a break. She's just arrived. Let her at least get a roof back on the place before you start demanding your favourite pastries."

Katie smiled, and the worry in her chest lifted a little.

Maybe they didn't want the pub to return to its previous state. "It's okay. I *do* plan on serving breakfasts. And yes to proper tea—I found boxes and boxes upstairs full of old teacups and teapots, all garish and mismatched. It gave me the idea to make it a theme of the new restaurant. I want to do both proper English tea and Chinese tea. I've got this idea for a sort of Kiwi-Asian fusion restaurant, because that's sort of what I grew up with and—" She realised she was rambling. She did that when she was excited about something. "Sorry."

"No! Don't be," said Ellen. "It's wonderful to see your enthusiasm. That tired old pub needs a makeover. I do have to ask, though, what you intend to do with the upstairs." She glanced at the other women and they all nodded.

"Well, obviously, the one end of that storey needs to be completely gutted because of fire damage. Have you been up on that floor?" Ellen nodded and Katie continued. "I had an engineer out last week, and he thinks I can knock out all the walls between the rooms to the right of the stairs and create one big room for functions. The rooms to the left of the stairs will become my office and a store room."

Ellen nodded. "May I suggest you use Room Four as the storeroom? And probably best to make sure there's a lock on the door."

"Why Room Four?" Katie asked. It seemed a strange thing to say.

"Smoke damage," Margaret replied. "It's really hard to get that smell out, and Room Four was the most damaged by the fire."

That made sense, although Katie hoped the smell wouldn't linger after all the renovations were complete.

Pauline nudged Sharon. "Well, we should be going or Jane will think we've abandoned her." Then she addressed Katie. "We're all members of a local gardening group. We meet a couple of times a month."

Katie perked up. "Oh! Maybe you can help me later on. I'd love to grow my own herbs and maybe some of the hard-to-find Chinese vegetables onsite."

The women all nodded enthusiastically. "We can probably even provide seeds and cuttings for you—between us, we grow almost every food plant possible to cultivate in this area," said Pauline.

Sharon chuckled. "And a few that aren't. Margaret's got pineapples growing in her greenhouse."

"Pineapples!" How did she manage that?

Margaret laughed. "Come on, ladies. Jane's waiting for us."

The women left, with promises to pop back around with seed, produce, jam and half a dozen other things they determined she needed. Katie blinked at their retreating backs, feeling like she'd just been swarmed by bees.

"I see you've met the Rifton Garden Group and survived." The voice behind Katie made her jump. She turned to see a man and a woman, about her age, approaching on foot through the side entrance to the car park. Did everyone walk in this town? And why were they all stopping by while she was filthy?

"Yeah. They're ..."

"Intense?" The woman smiled. "They're good people. My gran was part of that group until she passed away. Just don't get them started on the topic of compost unless you've got a couple of hours free."

The man smiled. "Hi. I'm Shelby Saunders. You can call me Shel."

"And I'm Alex Blackburn," the woman added.

Katie shook both their hands. "I'm Katie. Nice to meet you. Are you also walking past to spy on the new publican?"

The couple laughed. "Well, it did cross our minds," Alex said.

Shelby raised a hand. "I have a good excuse though. My great-grandparents owned this pub from nineteen fourteen to nineteen forty-five."

"Wow! Really?"

Shelby smiled. "Yeah. Apparently Mary, my great-grandmother, was an amazing brewer. Grew hops in her garden and brewed most of the beer the pub served."

"Cool. So does your family still brew?" To serve local beer would be awesome.

"Nah. But Pauline reckons she's growing hops that originally came from cuttings of Mary's hops plant."

"So, what are your plans for the pub?" Alex asked.

Katie really needed to work on an elevator speech about the pub. No doubt she was going to be asked this question by everyone in Rifton. She explained her vision, and then turned the conversation.

"So what do you two do?"

"I'm a game designer. I work for Scarlet Pimpernel," Shelby said.

"Scarlet Pimpernel? I love their games! It is so empowering to solve humanitarian crises instead of shooting zombies." Katie turned to Alex. "And you?"

"Well, I'm kind of between jobs. I've spent the past five years working for Biosecurity in Wellington. When Gran died a few months ago, I came back here to settle her estate and" — Alex and Shelby shared a look— "things got complicated."

Katie interpreted 'things got complicated' as 'Shel and I got involved'. She nodded, glancing between the two. Complicated. That's exactly how Katie would describe romantic relationships. After watching more than one kitchen romance explode in hurled knives and thrown pots of pasta, she'd sworn off that sort of complication. She didn't have time for it.

"Anyway, my inheritance included Gran's house and enough money to quit a job I didn't really like, so I've moved back to Rifton while I decide what I want to do next." She shrugged. "Not nearly as exciting as opening your own restaurant. Are you a chef?"

Katie nodded. "I've been sous chef at Brennan's in Christchurch for four years." *Four years*, and when the head chef position opened up recently, they hired fucking Dante for the position instead of promoting her. Just thinking about it made her chest hurt. She couldn't wait to quit.

"Are you living in Christchurch?" Alex asked.

"For now. Once the restaurant opens, though, I'll need to move closer. So if you know of any places for rent in Rifton or nearby, let me know."

"Will do," Shelby said. "It was nice to meet you. Good luck with the renovations. I'm sure we'll be seeing more of you." Alex and Shelby turned and resumed their walk.

Katie headed back inside. Just two more boxes to lug out, and the place would be ready for the renovators.

She stacked the final box in the shipping container and locked it, then dusted off her hands, which were dark with soot and grime. Turning back to survey the building once more, she took in the sagging roof and began to doubt the wisdom of this project. Fire or not, the building was a hundred and thirty years old. What would the renovators find when they started ripping off plaster and flooring? Would the bank even give her a business loan? If they did, would she ever be able to pay it back? What if it all went wrong?

Her phone buzzed, reminding her it was time to get back to town so she'd be ready in time for her shift at Brennan's. *Ugh.* She was exhausted already. How was she going to make it through her shift? She dreaded the night ahead.

She looked at the old pub again, this time seeing her ticket out of a shitty job, into a new phase in her life in which she was in control. Yeah. She'd make this thing work, no matter what.

# Interlude 1

## *1935*

Mary Saunders gave the wort one more swirl, reciting the brewer's spell that would ensure an excellent fermentation. There. That was the next batch of beer under way. And not a moment too soon—Thunder streaked into the room, his grey tail twitching and his ears flattened against his head.

*The maggot is screaming again.* Thunder's gravelly voice resounded in Mary's head.

Mary sighed. "I wish you wouldn't call him that. He's a baby, and his name is Dexter. He is not a maggot."

*Could have fooled me. White, hairless, ugly—*

"That's enough." Truly, she sympathised with her familiar, the demonic cat she'd summoned seventeen years ago. Dex was a fussy baby. Mary loved him, but even *she* sometimes wanted to pull her hair out when he wouldn't stop wailing. "Why don't you go see what Eunice is up to today? It's washing day—there may be some lovely white sheets to tear off the line and drag through the mud. You'll need to hurry, though. I want you to walk home from school with the children. Geoffrey Glandovy tried to pull Josephine into the bushes yesterday. If he so much as looks sideways at any of my girls again, I want him to pay for it."

*Can I drag him through the mud like the washing?* Thunder's entire reason for being here was to terrorise Eunice Glandovy, Geoffrey's mother. Mary had summoned Thunder in a rage after Eunice and her do-good prohibition promoters had thrown rocks through her windows. Although Thunder did lots of other things for Mary these days, harassing Eunice was his favourite. Really, anything involving causing someone pain seemed to please him. Mary tried to curb his bloodlust most of the time, but when it came to Eunice and her bully of a son, she sided with the demonic cat.

"Drag him through a gorse bush, too, while you're at it."

A deep, rumbling chuckle came from the demon's throat as he bounded out the door. Mary wiped her hands on her apron and went to see if she could settle Dex.

Later that afternoon, with Dex being cared for by the older girls, Mary walked to the pub to help Clive with the afternoon rush. Thunder trotted at her side, tail in the air, head held high.

"Dare I ask what you got up to today at the Glandovys' place?" she asked. "How are Mrs Glandovy's sheets looking?"

*No sheets; better than that. It was apparently underwear washing day,* the cat replied. *And someone had conveniently piled horse manure near the washing line.*

Mary snorted a laugh. "How did the walk home from school go?"

*A bit disappointing. The Glandovy brat turned tail and ran as soon as I hissed at him. I didn't even get to bite him.*

No doubt it was the glowing eyes that did the trick. Mary had talked to Thunder about that—it was disconcerting and led to uncomfortable questions Mary had to deflect—but he struggled to control it in the heat of the moment.

They arrived at the pub, and Mary stepped through the back door into the aromatic warmth of the kitchen.

"Mary!" Her husband Clive greeted her with a one-armed hug and a kiss on the cheek. With his other hand, he stirred a pan of onions sizzling in oil.

Mary took a deep breath, savouring the smells. "Steak, fish, and cheese and onion?" She guessed at the pie fillings Clive had made for this evening. He made the fillings, and she made the pastry. Together they'd fill the crusts and slide the pies into the big brick oven to bake. By the time five o'clock rolled around and the mad after-work rush came, the baking would be done and both Mary and Clive would frenetically serve beer and pies for an hour until their mandated six o'clock closing time.

Mary pulled on her apron and started mixing up pie dough, while Thunder went on his daily prowl around the kitchen, looking for mice and rats before vanishing into the dining room.

"Eunice put up her posters on the door again," Clive said as Mary worked butter into the flour in her bowl. "They made nice fire starters for the oven."

Mary laughed. "Maybe we should thank her for all

the fuel she supplies us. At least she's not standing at the door shouting at everyone who tries to come into the pub." During the war, when Clive was overseas, Eunice and her band of prohibitionists had made Mary's life hell. The fire had gone out of the prohibitionist movement, but Eunice's grudge against Mary had never dulled.

Of course, Mary stoked that grudge every chance she got. Eunice still didn't know why her laundry got shredded, her chickens were killed, her ducks decapitated—Thunder was discreet, giving her no proof Mary was behind the mayhem. But Eunice blamed her anyway.

The pub filled up quickly at five, and Mary smiled as beer and pies practically flew across the counter. Eunice was a complete sourpuss, but everyone else in town appreciated Mary's beer and Clive's pies. Before she knew it, Clive was calling, "Last call!" There was a flurry of last-minute orders, growlers to be filled to take home, and pies to wrap 'to take home to the missus'.

Five minutes later, the last footsteps stomped out the door, and Mary wiped the sweat off her brow. "Whew! That was busy, even for a Friday."

Clive nodded. "I hope the girls are cooking tonight, because there's not a single pie left."

"I left a pot of stew simmering on the—" the yowl of a cat upstairs was followed by scuffling and thumping. A door banged and the man who was staying in Room Four stumbled down the steps, with Thunder on his heels, hissing and snarling.

"What the hell is going on?" Clive asked.

Mary glared at Thunder, but the cat didn't take his eyes off the man.

"That bloody cat! It bit me."

*He was summoning a demon, and what he was calling was not something you want getting loose around here,* Thunder growled in Mary's head.

Summoning! Mary's gaze snapped to the man. There was nothing remarkable about him. Mary hadn't even looked twice when he arrived yesterday. It was shearing season, and he looked like all the other shearers who came through each year looking for work.

Clive stepped out from behind the bar and shooed Thunder away. "Sorry about the cat. I'm not sure what got into him—he's usually not aggressive."

Clive didn't know Thunder was a demon. After Mary's grandmother had been killed for suspected witchcraft, the women in the family kept their magic use quiet. Not that witches were burnt at the stake these days, but secrecy was easier than explaining the truth. Clive thought Thunder was nothing but a particularly long-lived cat Mary had gotten for companionship during the war.

So Mary couldn't tell Clive why Thunder had bitten the man. Clive would smooth things over, and this man would go back to his summoning. How could Mary convince the man to leave? As Clive continued to apologise, offering the man a beer to compensate for the disturbance, Thunder arrowed up the steps.

Mary slipped out from behind the bar and made her way upstairs to catch up to him. She found him sitting outside the door to Room Four, tail thrashing.

"He's only supposed to be here until tomorrow," she whispered. "Can you keep an eye on him until then?"

*What? Am I nothing but a babysitter now?*

"Well, I can't exactly spend the night in his room,

can I? Either we kick him out—and I don't know how to justify it to Clive—or you keep an eye on him so he doesn't try it again."

Thunder harrumphed. After a moment, he said, *Let me into the room. The only thing his summoning will bring out is my claws.*

"Thank you." Mary eased the door open, mindful of the squeak of hinges.

*You owe me extra fish tomorrow.*

Mary rolled her eyes. "Fine. Now go before he comes back up."

Thunder sauntered into the room and Mary closed the door behind him.

# Chapter 4

## *A Celebration*

Katie pulled open the door of The Witch's Brew, her stomach churning with a mixture of elation and terror. Stepping out of Brennan's for the last time today had felt incredible, but submitting her business registration later in the day sent a spike of fear through her. There was no backing out now. She owned her own restaurant, and opening day was fast approaching. This evening was supposed to be a celebration of that fact, but Katie's brain spun with all the daunting tasks before her now that she'd made the leap.

"Your aunt is meeting us here?" Tui asked as they both stepped into the cosy bar.

Katie nodded. "I told her she's buying the drinks, too, since she's the one responsible for me quitting my job and starting this crazy restaurant venture."

Tui laughed. "What does she look like?"

"Well, last time I saw her, she had acid green hair, but since she changes colours every couple of weeks, I'm not sure."

"Is that her, the carrot top?" Tui pointed to a table on the left side of the room.

The woman, sitting alone and scrolling through her phone, had bright orange hair, cut in a short bob. She wore a fitted orange jumpsuit with a rhinestone-crusted belt and silver flats. "Oh my god. She looks like a road cone. Yep. That's Aunt Rachael."

"I don't know ... somehow she's rocking OSH orange. Is she as wacky as she looks?" Tui muttered through a grin.

"More so," Katie replied as they walked over to Aunt Rachael's table.

Rachael looked up as they approached. "Katie-pie!" Her face split into a grin and she stood to wrap Katie in a hi-vis hug. "Congratulations on quitting your job!"

Katie hugged Rachael back. Her aunt was a complete nut, but she was loads of fun. Katie and Tui sat down at Rachael's table, and Katie introduced her aunt and her friend to one another.

Rachael picked up a drinks menu. "So, what'll it be tonight? Katie says I'm buying, so go wild."

The Witch's Brew was famous for its cocktails, all of which had witchy names, most based on the famous cauldron scene in *Macbeth*. Katie studied the menu. "Oh, I think I have to start with Eye of Newt." It was her favourite—essentially a martini, with a bit of spirulina to give it a green colour and earthy flavour. A green olive sitting in the bottom of the glass was the *eye of newt* for which it was named.

"True," Tui said. "Which means I should order Toe of Frog."

"I suppose it's Wool of Bat for me, then," Rachael said. "I mean, if we're drinking them in order." She chuckled. "We going to drink them all?"

Tui hooted a laugh. "All fifteen? Yeah, bring it on! Katie's done with that shitty job—let's party!"

Uh oh. Katie wasn't sure she wanted to get wasted. "Let's just see how we go, eh?"

"Party pooper." Tui stuck her tongue out at Katie.

They ordered their drinks, and then Rachael leaned

forward. "So, tell me about your plans for the pub."

"Well, it'll be Kiwi-Asian fusion. I'm thinking of the sort of things Mum used to make for us kids growing up—scallion pancakes with golden syrup, pavlova with durian and lychee, lamb and mint spring rolls ... I've got heaps of ideas. I just need to pare them down to finalise the menu."

"Sounds great! What are your plans for the upstairs?"

"The renovators are knocking out a couple of walls between rooms to make a function room I'll rent out for birthday parties, work functions and the like. And I'll use a room for my office and one for storage." Katie grimaced. "It's not the nicest space—the ceilings are a little low—but the builder is installing larger windows that will at least make the rooms lighter. Hopefully once it's all painted and well lit, it won't feel quite so ... dingy."

"Find anything interesting while you were cleaning out and tearing up carpets?" Aunt Rachael raised her eyebrows expectantly.

Katie smiled. "Actually, yeah. Tui and I found all these old teacups and teapots in boxes in one of the upstairs rooms. And I thought, how perfect is that? Tea is such a Chinese *and* Kiwi thing. I figured I'd run with that as a theme for the restaurant."

"What a great idea! Find anything else?"

"What did you think I'd find, a pot of gold?" Had Aunt Rachael left something there for her to find?

Rachael laughed. "No. I've just heard that the Rifton Pub was ... quirky."

No wonder Rachael had bought it. "Well, other than the teacups, there wasn't anything quirky in the building. Just a lot of rubbish—I don't think the place has been renovated for fifty years."

Tui broke in. "It's gonna be amazing once it's fully

renovated, and you're going to wow them with your food, Katie. Rifton isn't going to know what hit it."

"I *am* worried that in a small town like Rifton, the Kiwi-Asian fusion idea might not go over well, though. You know how ... Pākehā, white, those places can be."

"You'll win them over, no doubt," Rachael said, leaning back as the server brought their drinks.

Katie picked up her Eye of Newt and sipped the murky green liquid as she turned her plans over in her head. The few people she'd met in Rifton had been receptive to the idea of a Kiwi-Asian fusion restaurant, at least to her face. But no doubt there would be others who wanted a classic Kiwi pub. Would there be enough supporters to make it work? Or would the place flounder? It wasn't a location she'd *choose* to start a restaurant in if it hadn't fallen into her lap.

Still, her restaurant didn't need to make her rich. If she could make this one work financially, someday she could sell it and buy a place in a trendy neighbourhood somewhere. It was her *first* restaurant. It didn't have to be perfect, right?

"What's wrong?" Tui asked.

"Huh?" Katie shook herself out of her ruminations.

"You're thinking about something. I can see it on your face."

Katie huffed out a breath. "Just nervous about the restaurant. Worried I won't be able to make it work."

"Katie, you've got this. You're an amazing cook," Aunt Rachael said. "It's why I gave you the place."

"Owning a restaurant isn't the same as being a cook. I've got to worry about staffing, payroll, finances, renovations ... everything."

"And you'll do fine," Tui said. "You're, like, the most organised person I know. You'll have everything sorted weeks before opening, and you'll be an amazing boss. I can't wait to work for you."

"Are you sure you want to work for me? I mean, we've been friends for forever. What if I don't manage to make this work and I have to fire you? It'll be awful. You'll hate me."

"Katie, relax. You won't have to fire me, and if you do, I'll know why and I won't hate you. I'll just take some time off and make lots of art while I look for another job." Tui did mixed-media work that incorporated found objects, documents, newspaper clippings, and other strange items into wry observations on modern life. She'd taken several boxes of stuff from the old pub to use in new works.

"You say that now, but—"

"Stop. You're going to create the best restaurant in the South Island. End of discussion." Tui slammed back the last of her drink. "Now, have you thought about your logo yet?"

Katie laughed. "I'm still trying to get my head around the renovation plan."

"Good. I have some ideas." Tui pulled a sketchbook from her purse and flipped it open to a page of sketches. Teapots, teacups, baked goods, pies ...

Katie and Rachael both leaned over for a better look.

"You've been working on my logo?" Warmth filled Katie's chest. Tui was an amazing artist, and Katie would have eventually asked her to create her restaurant's logo, but she probably wouldn't have thought about it until weeks before opening.

"Of course I have. And before you say anything, I'm not doing it for free—I want to be able to hang my art on your walls—sell it in the restaurant." Tui's confidence faltered for a moment and she flashed a sheepish smile. "I mean, if that's okay with you."

Katie smiled. "That's a fabulous idea! Of course you can!" She could easily envision Tui's big, quirky pieces hanging around the dining room of her restaurant.

Tui's smile broadened. "Okay, so I've done a bunch of sketches here, but until I know what you're going to call the restaurant, it's hard to come up with something that's right."

"So, what *are* you going to call it?" Rachael asked.

Katie had only just decided a few hours ago when she submitted her business application. She still wasn't entirely convinced it was the right name. But when she told Rachael and Tui what she'd decided, Tui's face lit up.

"Oh! Wait! I have an idea." She slipped a pencil from her purse and flipped to a clean page in the sketchbook. Her shoulders hunched as the pencil flew across the page. The drawing pulled together elements from her previous ideas, and brought Katie's restaurant name to life. How did she manage that? And how did Katie get so lucky as to have an aunt who would buy her a freaking *restaurant* and a friend who was so talented?

"Oh my god. That's perfect!" The worry in Katie's stomach dissipated, replaced with eager anticipation. She was really doing this!

# Chapter 5

## *The Tipsy Teapot*

Katie made one last circuit of the building before opening the doors to her very first customers. She had met her pastry chef, Jill, at four o'clock this morning, and the smell of their early morning baking permeated the dining area—cinnamon, sugar, yeast. Within an hour, savoury smells would start wafting out of the kitchen from lunch preparations. Hopefully all the wonderful aromas would encourage people to splurge.

Katie's sneakers squeaked on the newly finished kauri floorboards—who would have thought this beautiful floor existed underneath three layers of old linoleum? Each table was topped with a teacup holding sugar packets, old-fashioned china salt and pepper shakers, and menus featuring the logo Tui had designed for her—a china teapot tipped on an angle, with tea sloshing out—and the name of her new restaurant, The Tipsy Teapot. She smiled and ran her fingers lightly over a menu.

Laughter echoed from the kitchen, where her staff were hard at work on the pies, sandwiches, spring rolls and other goodies that would fill the lunch menu. The sound brought a smile to her face. She would not run a kitchen where people were put down, where staff were bullied and made to feel they were dispensable. Where people were fired for making a mistake or calling in sick. Hopefully the laughter was a sign she'd gotten off on the right foot.

Alex and Shel walked past on the footpath, headed for the door, and Katie snapped into action. Customers! It was time to open the doors.

She glanced back at her barista, Neil. He gave her a thumbs up and a smile. With one final scan of the room to ensure everything was in order, Katie unlocked the door.

"Yay! We're the first," Alex said as she stepped in. She glanced around the room. "Wow! You've done such an amazing job with this place!"

Katie smiled. "Thanks. I just hope it does well."

"I'm sure it will—the old pub was busy all the time, and this is much nicer than it used to be."

"Best of all, there's breakfast." Shel rubbed his hands together. "Come on, let's order before the rush. I want to try the breakfast dumplings with maple syrup."

Alex and Shelby ordered and took their seats. By the time Neil had delivered their coffees, another six people had arrived.

Business was steady, but not manic, through the morning. Perfect for their first day—it allowed them to work out the kinks in their system.

The garden group showed up during the mid-afternoon lull for a late lunch. Pauline left her signature gumboots at the door, but carried a potted plant. She set it down on the bar, which Katie was staffing while Neil took a break. Katie raised her eyebrows at the dirt that spilled onto the polished surface. Onto her beautiful new bar.

Pauline nodded at the plant. "I thought you should have a lime tree."

"So you can make gin and tonics with your own limes,"

Margaret added.

Katie smiled. "Aw, that's sweet of you."

Margaret extracted a smaller plant from her oversized purse. Katie recognised it as rosemary. "I didn't pot this up," Margaret explained as she handed over the plant, with its roots wrapped in damp newspaper. "You'll want to get it into the ground pretty quickly, or pot it if you're not ready to plant it out."

"Thank you." Katie took the proffered plant and set it in the sink behind the bar.

Ellen was next. She handed over a purple sage plant. "That'll go well in your pumpkin and feta pie."

Jane gave Katie a milk bottle filled with a dark liquid. Katie frowned at it, and Jane laughed. "That's worm wee."

"It's what?" Katie held the bottle further from her body.

"Worm wee—it's great fertiliser for the garden. You'll want to especially use it on that lime. They're heavy feeders."

All right then. Katie set the bottle on the floor. No way was she putting worm wee on the counter.

Sharon handed over a small brown envelope with the words *Chinese Broccoli* handwritten on it. "I don't know if this is really a Chinese vegetable, but I know it's delicious and hard to find in the supermarkets so I thought you might like to grow it. These are seeds I collected from my plants last year."

Katie smiled. "Yes! We call it gai lan. I haven't had it in ages. Thank you." Her smile faded. "But I don't know how to grow it."

Sharon explained how to start the seeds in an ice cream tub filled with soil, and then set them out in the garden.

"Thank you." In spite of the dirt on the bar and the obvious violation of the health code, Katie was touched by the women's thoughtfulness. "Are you here to eat?" she asked hopefully.

"Absolutely!" Pauline said. The women perused the items in the cabinet.

Sharon gave a cheer. "You've got carrot cake!"

Katie laughed. "How could I not have carrot cake after you asked specifically for it?" She wasn't confident her cake was perfect—she wasn't a big carrot cake fan herself, but she knew what she did like in carrot cake—plenty of spices, sultanas and ginger along with the carrots. "You'll have to tell me if it's up to your standards."

Then the women all placed their orders and sat down at a table by the window. As Katie fixed their coffees, the sound of their conversation wafted across the dining area. Katie wasn't eavesdropping, and she didn't catch all of what they said, but she heard the words *compost* and *weeds* so she knew they were talking gardening.

When she brought their coffees to their table, Margaret asked, "What's that unusual plant you've planted at the back of the car park? The one with those large, toothed leaves."

Katie shook her head. "I haven't planted anything yet. I've been focused on getting the restaurant ready for opening. Figured I'd worry about the landscaping later."

"Hmm. I don't remember seeing them before, do you?" Jane asked the others.

They all shook their heads, and Pauline said, "Well, there used to be a big skip back there. They were probably hidden behind the skip."

When Neil returned from his break, he forced Katie to take her first breather for the day. "Get out of here for at least thirty minutes. Eat something. You've been going non-stop since the butt crack of dawn."

Katie laughed. "I think four am counts as *before* the butt crack of dawn."

"Exactly. Now go away and take a rest. We've got this."

Once again, Katie was filled with the sense she was starting off right with her staff. She couldn't imagine anyone at Brennan's telling the head chef or owner to take a break. She put up her hands in surrender. "Okay, okay. I'm going." She snatched a pie out of the cabinet and filled a glass with ice water. Then she headed out back to the picnic table she'd set up for employee breaks on the postage-stamp-sized scrap of lawn between the building and the car park. It was a relief to sink down onto the bench. God, did her feet hurt! She should be used to it, but then maybe feet weren't meant to have no breaks for eleven hours straight.

The breeze cooled her sweaty skin and flipped a loose lock of hair into her eyes. She tucked her hair behind her ear and then bit into the pie, savouring the gooey cheese and earthy mushrooms. It was her personal recipe, but had been made by Jill this morning. It was absolutely divine. Or maybe Katie was simply ravenous. When was the last time she'd had anything to eat? Must have been before four this morning.

When the pie was gone, she sipped her water and scanned the unkempt shrubbery around the car park—the remains of a poorly kept hedge. She planned on turning all the area into gardens at some stage. Maybe the women from the garden group could recommend a gardener. Katie sure as hell wasn't one. Even if she had the time, she knew nothing about cultivating plants—she just liked the idea of building menus around seasonal produce grown onsite.

A cluster of bright green, large-leafed plants at the back of the car park caught her eye. Were those the plants Margaret had asked about? They certainly looked different from all the others. With a groan, Katie heaved herself up and strolled over to take a closer look.

There were four of them, about waist height. Most of

their leaves were about the size and shape of Katie's hand, but at the tip of each branch were a pair of sickle-shaped leaves with jagged edges facing one another. She laughed—they looked like crab claws.

Walking along the edge of the car park, Katie surveyed the rest of the scraggly plants. Someone had kept them hacked back, but they were a sad lot. She couldn't identify many of them. There were a few that looked like pine trees, several with big waxy leaves she thought must have once been attractive, and a mishmash of others. All of them were shot through with rank grasses and gorse. There was nothing worth saving.

A car pulled into the car park and disgorged a family of five. Then another one arrived with two couples. It looked like the afternoon lull was over; she should get back inside. On her way in, she met the garden group coming out.

"How was your meal?" she asked.

"It was excellent." Pauline beamed, and the others echoed her words.

"That mushroom pie is to die for!" Sharon said.

"And the carrot cake?"

Sharon's face grew thoughtful. "The cake itself was great—I like the ginger in it. I think you could work on your frosting, though. It's not quite right."

Frosting, eh? "Well, I'll have to do some testing. I hope you're willing to try it again."

"Oh yes!" Sharon's smile lit up again. "It was very good."

"Just not quite perfect?"

"Exactly."

Katie laughed to herself as she stepped back inside. Those women were a hoot.

Tui arrived for her shift shortly after Katie returned to work, coming in through the front entrance and gazing around the busy dining room. "I couldn't wait to get here!

Look at it, hopping with customers!"

Katie handed Tui an apron. Tui held it up and squealed. "You put the logo on our aprons!"

"And on the staff shirts. There's a selection of sizes in the break room. Go choose your size."

Tui hurried upstairs with a smile, returning a few minutes later outfitted in a crisp new Tipsy Teapot T-shirt. She rubbed her hands together. "Okay, let's get started!" Without prompting, she initiated the handover of the register from Livia, and began ringing up customers, enquiring cheerfully how their meal was and encouraging them to return again.

If they could keep up this level of enthusiasm, they'd do great.

The remainder of the day passed in a whirlwind. Katie worked in the kitchen alongside her staff until she was certain they had things under control, and then she floated between jobs, taking a turn at every one to get a feel for how their systems were working. There were tweaks to be made—at the height of the busy dinner seating, she had to pull her dishwasher in as a runner, because food wasn't getting to the tables fast enough, and then one of her line cooks had to switch to dishwashing when they ran out of clean plates. But things settled down around eight o'clock, and they cruised along with a crowd of locals happy to enjoy the new pub until closing time at ten.

When the last of her staff finally hung up their aprons and waved farewell, Katie locked the doors and headed home to her new house—a tiny cottage she'd found for rent just two blocks from the pub. It had seemed close, but tonight, with aching feet and exhaustion dragging her down, it felt like miles away.

Still, a sense of accomplishment buoyed her up—she'd done it! She'd opened her own restaurant. She'd have to thank Aunt Rachael again, for real this time. Maybe a burnt-out pub was exactly what she'd needed for her birthday.

# Interlude 2

## *1946*

Mary reached for the handle of the pub's kitchen door, then drew her hand back. It was hard to break the habit of coming and going through the back. But the pub wasn't hers anymore. The thought still made her want to set Thunder loose on a government official somewhere. After all those years of running this place with Clive, and then running it on her own all through the war, brewing the best beer in the South Island, it was snatched from her, just days after Clive's funeral.

Clive had specifically given her the pub in his will, and that wasn't a problem. It was the liquor licence that caused Mary grief. Three days after she buried her husband, a letter arrived from the local liquor licensing committee, headed by Eunice Glandovy's brother.

*It has come to the attention of the Liquor Licensing Committee that, upon the death of Clive Saunders, the Rifton Pub ownership has passed to you. As a woman, it is unlawful for you to hold a liquor licence unless you have obtained the necessary protection order upon the death of your husband. As you have failed to obtain a protection order, in accordance with the Alcoholic Liquors Sale Control Act of 1893, we hereby revoke your liquor licence, effective immediately.*

It was true, she hadn't obtained a protection order. How could she have? How was she to know Clive would pass away so quickly? There should have been some sort of grace period, shouldn't there? But the law didn't include one, so she had no choice but to stop brewing and sell the pub.

Eunice had been unbearably smug. "Oh you poor dear, Mary. What will you do now?" She didn't even try to hide her glee at finally getting the better of Mary.

Mary had sent Thunder on a campaign of destruction against Eunice's prizewinning poultry, but even a year later, the loss of the pub burned in her chest.

Walking around to the front, she stepped into the familiar space and was greeted with warm hellos by all her old regular patrons. Their support, while incapable of changing the outcome of Clive's death, meant everything to her.

Sean Fraser, the new publican, called out from behind the bar. "Mary! Pint on the house?"

Mary waved away the offer—it wasn't her beer, and besides, "I've just come looking for Thunder. He's vanished again."

Thunder apparently didn't care that Mary no longer owned the pub. He still acted as though it was *his* establishment.

"He was skulking around the kitchen earlier," Sean said. "Honest, I don't mind him—he's an excellent mouser. Yesterday, he even nabbed a rat in the storeroom."

"All well and good," Mary said. "But I'd rather he caught mice in my kitchen. You can get your own cat."

"How old is that animal, anyway?" Freddie Parsons asked. "I remember him following at your heels back when I was in primary school."

Yes, a twenty-eight-year-old cat was strange. "Oh, you're thinking of the first grey cat I had. I called him Thunder, too. I suppose I don't have much imagination when it comes to names. Now, I need to find that cat and get home before Dex returns from school, or the boy will conveniently forget his chores."

Sean waved a hand towards the stairs. "No doubt he's upstairs. There's no one in Room Four."

Sure enough, the furry demon was curled up on the bed in Room Four. He opened one eye and glared at Mary when she came in.

*I'm not bothering anyone here. Let me be.*

"Why do you insist upon coming here?"

Thunder huffed as he stood and stretched.

*I like it here. The bed is softer than yours.*

Mary narrowed her eyes at him, certain his gravitation towards Room Four had nothing to do with the bed. "Well, you can't keep coming here. This isn't my pub anymore, and at some point, you'll push Mr Fraser's patience too far."

*I'll go wherever the hell I please.*

Thunder leapt off the bed and strutted, tail in the air, out of the room. Mary rolled her eyes and followed him out.

# Chapter 6

## Date Night

"I'm looking forward to seeing what Katie's got on the dinner menu," Alex said as she and Shelby walked to the Tipsy Teapot on a Friday night in late October.

"Yeah, I can't believe we've waited this long to come down for dinner," Shel replied. "Of course, I *do* like the breakfast menu. A lot."

Alex laughed. "Well, now that I'm working again, we'll have to come down for dinners instead of breakfasts." Assuming, of course, that they'd continue to come to the Tipsy Teapot together.

The restaurant was hopping when they stepped in the door. It was like an entirely different place from the breakfast scene they'd experienced over the past three weeks—different lighting, different music, and different staff, too. Instead of small-town cosy, the vibe was more city chic.

"Alex! Shelby!" Katie strode across the room towards them. "This isn't your normal time."

Alex laughed. "We're celebrating my new job."

"Oh! Congratulations! Where are you working?"

"I'm the new Biodiversity Officer at the district council, which means I'll be staying in Rifton."

"Awesome! Well, grab yourselves a table—dinner menus

are there, and it's order at the bar, like breakfast."

They found a table by the windows and opened their menus.

"I'm buying—order whatever you'd like," Shelby said.

"You don't have to pay for my dinner. I'm the one with a new job—I should be buying tonight."

"Nonsense. I'm the one who asked you out."

Alex lifted her eyes from her menu. Was this a date? When Shel had suggested they go to the Tipsy Teapot to celebrate her new job, it sounded casual. *Hey, we should celebrate with dinner at Katie's place, I want to see what her dinner menu is like anyway.* She watched Shel peruse his menu. He didn't look at her.

They'd spent a fair bit of time together lately—he helped her tear up the old carpet in Gran's house, and he showed up regularly with treats for Gran's 'cat', Thor. Thor wasn't really a cat; he was a demon, *Felis daemonicus,* from the summoning book Gran had left behind when she died. Thor and Shelby had seemingly bonded, and Alex sometimes joked that the cat was the only reason Shel visited her.

Despite the time they spent together, Alex hadn't felt the sort of intimacy with Shel that she'd felt before, when they were racing to banish the demon Alex accidentally summoned back in the autumn. There had been no late nights together, no falling asleep on the couch together.

No giant pet-eating demonic centipedes, either, for which Alex was thankful. But now and again, she was nostalgic for those frantic, terror-filled days.

She returned her attention to the menu. Whatever. They were definitely friends, and probably more than friends. And now she was staying here in Rifton, they could take it as slow as they wanted.

They ordered burgers, chips and beer. Alex thought Katie

had been astute in her choice of dinner offerings; there seemed to be something for everyone, from classic Kiwi fare to exotic-sounding Asian dishes.

The restaurant continued to fill as Alex and Shelby enjoyed their dinner. Every table was full, and there were two groups at the bar, waiting for space to open up.

"Katie has done such a great job with this place," Shelby said.

"She has. I hope she stays in Rifton; I heard the lease on her house is only for a year, while the owners are in Europe."

Alex took a bite of the bright green grilled asparagus that came with her burger. She wasn't a huge fan of asparagus in general, but these spears were rich and salty and sweet. Had they been marinated in something? "Oh my god. These are amazing," she said with her mouth full.

"So, you haven't told me much about how your first week went," Shelby prompted.

Alex swallowed before answering. "Yeah, it was full-on. They want me to do more outreach than I thought. I'm supposed to create a Selwyn Biodiversity website where I'll blog about things like rat trapping, planting for wildlife and stuff. I'm fine with the blogging, but it's going to be a steep learning curve to create a website."

"I can help you with the website. Easy-peasy." Shel dipped a hot chip into the pottle of aioli in the centre of the table.

"It's my job, Shel, not yours." Alex smiled. It was sweet of him to offer.

"No, really. I'm happy to help."

"You don't need to help; I'll figure it out."

"Right, so you'll accept my dubious assistance with home renovation, but not my expert computer help?" He laughed. "Alex, I'm a computer geek living with his parents—who else is more qualified to help you create a website?"

Alex smiled. "Okay, okay. You can help me with the website." She dipped a chip in aioli and popped it into her mouth. Meeting his gaze, she added, "Thanks."

He smiled. "My pleasure."

They didn't linger once they'd finished their meals—there were even more people waiting for tables, and they felt they should leave so someone else could sit down.

Alex zipped her jacket as they stepped outside. The day had been warm, but it was breezy and cool now. The sun was long set, but the sky was still tinged dusty pink. "Thanks for dinner," she said to Shelby as he exited behind her.

"My pleasure. Congratulations on your new job. We'll have to come back some evening when it's not so crowded."

"My treat next time."

They strolled across the car park, angling towards the footpath. Alex took a deep breath as a sweet scent wafted past. "Wow! You smell that?" Without waiting for Shel's response, she veered towards the smell. "Look at these flowers!" At the edge of the car park was a cluster of shrubs as tall as her. Red, trumpet-shaped flowers hung below big, bright green leaves.

"Forget the flowers, look at those leaves!" Shelby said, his finger tracing the air in front of a pair of sickle-shaped leaves with serrated edges. "They're like ... crab claws or something."

"Are those spines?" As Alex asked the question, a gust of wind shook the bush, and the leaves whipped around. Shel jerked his hand back with a yelp.

"It bit me!" Shel clutched his right index finger.

Alex giggled. She was feeling light-headed. Maybe she should have stuck to one beer, not two. "It did not. It's a plant."

"Okay, so maybe the plant didn't *bite*, but it hurt. Look." Shel held out his finger. A drop of blood welled up from a small scratch.

Alex took his hand, turning it to get a closer look. "It's a scratch. But those leaves *are* like crab claws." She giggled and tugged him a little further from the plant.

"Maybe the plants are actually crabs." Shelby snorted a laugh. Then he narrowed his eyes at them. "Did that one move?"

Yeah, both of them might have had too much to drink. Alex tugged on Shel's hand again. "Come on. Let's go. We can ask Katie about the plants tomorrow."

As they turned, they nearly bumped shoulders with a couple walking arm in arm across the car park.

"Oops. Sorry," Alex said. But the couple were oblivious, focused on each other.

"I hope you're planning to take me home tonight," said the woman, gazing up at the guy.

"Oh yeah, babe. You're staying *all* night," he replied.

Alex struggled to hide her giggle at the exchange. But then Shel suddenly turned serious and grasped her arms. "Come home with me."

She blinked at him. Was he suggesting ...? She wondered if his parents were at home tonight. Though she felt light headed, a part of her brain thought it didn't make sense. If he *was* suggesting what she thought he was, then *her* place would be much better.

"Maybe my place instead? You know ... your folks ..."

Shel nodded and wrapped his arm around her as he hurriedly bundled her towards home.

Ten minutes later, as she unlocked her front door with Shel on her heels, Alex felt weird about the situation. Not about having Shel at her place—she was perfectly comfortable with that. But thinking back to standing in the car park at the Tipsy Teapot, she'd felt drunk. And Shel had *acted* drunk.

She stepped into the kitchen and flicked the kettle on out of habit before turning to face him. As she opened her mouth to speak, Shel beat her to it.

"Look, Alex, I'm sorry. I don't know what ... I mean, I ..."

"Did you feel as drunk as I did back there in the car park?" she asked.

He looked relieved. "Yes. I don't know why. Normally, two beers wouldn't hit me like that. Now that my head is a bit clearer, I didn't want you to feel like, like I was pressuring you or anything, or taking advantage of you while you were drunk. You know, I—"

"Did you not want to come back here?" As much as Alex felt the same about having been drunk, she was a bit disappointed that they were both feeling more sober and rational.

A sheepish smile crept over Shel's face. "I didn't say that. I just didn't want you to feel pressured."

Alex smiled back. "Well, then. How about I make some tea while you find us a movie to watch on Netflix?"

# Chapter 7

## *Strike One*

Saturday morning, Katie was in the kitchen early with her pastry chef, Jill. "What do you think of this frosting?" she asked Jill, scooping a teaspoon full of the creamy confection out of the mixing bowl and handing it to her.

"Sharon still hasn't approved, eh?" Jill asked as she took the spoon. "You know you don't have to—"

"Are you kidding? Giving Sharon the perfect carrot cake frosting is a personal mission now." The garden group came for morning tea nearly every Saturday now, and Sharon always got the carrot cake. Katie asked her every time how she liked it, and every time Sharon told her it wasn't quite perfect. Katie knew it wasn't bad—the lack of perfection didn't stop Sharon from ordering it the following week and eating every last crumb. Katie even caught her last week licking the plate. But it was a game Katie was enjoying.

Jill swirled the frosting around in her mouth for a moment, then licked her lips. "It's good. There's more of a sour note to it than the last batch."

Katie nodded. "I added some lemon juice."

"And it didn't get too thin?"

"I had to compensate with a little more sugar. Hopefully it will still stay soft and not crust over too much."

Jill handed the spoon back. "Give it a go. It's good. See what Sharon thinks."

Four hours later, Katie made an appearance at the garden group's table as they were finishing up. "Katie! How are you this week? Has business been good?" they all chimed in.

Katie nodded. "It was busier this week than last. I think the good weather helped. Lots of people spent the day in the mountains and stopped in afterwards for dinner. How was your food?"

"The miso and onion scone was better than I expected," Ellen said.

"And your carrot cake?" she asked Sharon.

Sharon smiled. "It was excellent ... but ... something about—"

"The frosting," the other women chorused.

"What? I'm serious. I liked the tartness of it, but it was a little grainy or something. And maybe too sweet? Can frosting be too sweet and tart at the same time?"

That extra sugar to compensate for the lemon juice. "Well, I suppose I have to keep working on it, then." Would yogurt provide the tartness without the need for extra sugar? Or maybe sour cream? Katie considered her options as she returned to the kitchen.

Saturday night, Taine, Katie's bartender, called in sick, so Katie was behind the bar for the evening filling in for him. She didn't mind—there was something Zen about tending bar, and it gave her an excuse to occasionally have a few words with customers, because she could pour drinks and chat at the same time. It also kept her in a central location, so that she could keep an eye on both kitchen and dining areas.

Mark Levitt had been regaling her with tales of farming in the 1970s for the past hour as he nursed his regular Saturday afternoon beer. He never ordered more than a beer, but she always made sure to slip him a strawberry tart, an asparagus roll, or some other little item made with the fresh produce he supplied to the Tipsy Teapot.

He tipped back the last swallow of beer and set the glass down with a heavy finality. Six o'clock—you could set a watch by that man. "Well, the missus is waiting," he said.

Katie smiled. "And she runs the farm," she replied, because it was exactly what he said every Saturday at six o'clock.

"It's been a pleasure, my dear. See you next week. Stay beautiful."

Katie's smile grew. "You're bringing more strawberries on Tuesday, right?"

"Wouldn't miss it." He settled his hat on his head and strolled out the door, greeting other patrons on his way out. Katie watched him go, smiling and shaking her head at the man—he could charm the fur off a cat. He reminded her of her dad.

As Mark stepped out the door, a younger man stepped in. He was tall, with dirty blond hair and a scruffy beard. The sleeves of his button-down shirt were rolled up, and his whole air was ever so slightly dishevelled.

"Damn. Look at him." Tui, on the register, paused.

Katie swatted her with a tea towel. "Back to work, you!" They both laughed.

As Katie's eyes swung back towards the approaching man, her smile lingered, and when his eyes met hers, she realised it was probably the wrong smile for a customer. She dropped her eyes and schooled her face into a polite bartender face before raising them again.

He didn't smile, but walked right up to the bar and sat down across from where Katie stood. Tui coughed pointedly from the register.

Katie wiped the bar with the towel in her hand, though it was perfectly clean. "What can I get you this evening, sir?"

"What have you got on tap?"

Katie rattled off the beers on offer, and he chose an IPA from a local microbrewery.

"Good choice." She wasn't overly fond of it, but it was popular. He laid his credit card on the card reader to pay, and Katie snuck a peek at the name—F G Laird. "I haven't seen you here before. Are you local?" she asked as she drew his beer.

"Darfield."

"And what brings you to the Tipsy Teapot from Darfield?" Most people were still in the 'I was curious about the new pub' phase, but she'd started to have a few that had heard good reviews from friends that drew them in.

He shrugged. "It was on my way home."

Right. Well. That was fine, too. She handed him his beer. "Enjoy. Let me know if you'd like anything else. We've got a great dinner selection." She reached for a menu and set it in front of him.

"Thanks," he said into his beer.

He drank slowly, with a frown on his face the whole time. Katie kept half an eye on him as she served other customers. After twenty minutes or so, with his beer only a third gone, she returned to him. "Everything okay here?" She asked brightly. "Can I get you some chips to go with that beer? Or maybe some of our spring rolls? They go really well with the bitter in the beer."

He shook his head, then returned his attention to his beer. Half an hour later, he slipped away while Katie's back was turned to fetch more ice.

"Well, that was a disappointment," Tui commented. "Bit of a stick up his arse."

Katie rolled her eyes. "He was fine. He bought a beer. There's no requirement to be chatty."

"The man didn't even look at you. I'd consider that a personal challenge, if I were you."

"He didn't look at you, either. Do *you* consider that a challenge?"

"I'm not single. Seriously girl, back at uni, you would have been all over that guy. No way would you have taken that surly shit from him."

This was the problem with hiring old friends. They knew you when you were young and foolish. "He was a *customer*, Tui. A customer."

The rest of the night was busy. Katie lost track of what was going on in the kitchen and dining room, trusting her staff to take care of things, trusting them to let her know if they needed her. The early drinkers gave way to the dinner drinkers, then the partying drinkers. She kept an eye on the group of eight twenty-somethings who seemed to be celebrating a birthday. She'd deliberately priced her beer high enough to discourage binge drinking, and this group, while loud and boisterous, had only downed three rounds over the last two hours when word came of a commotion outside.

"A fight?" she asked when Lane, one of her line cooks who'd been out having a break, came to tell her.

"Yeah. In the car park."

"Do we need to ring the police?"

A customer who'd just left stepped back through the door and tapped another man on the shoulder. Lane nodded towards the men. "No need. That's Dale Smith, one of the local constables."

"Should I go out there?"

"Nah. Dale will sort it out. If he needs you, he'll let you know."

Katie frowned. A fight. At her bar. She cast her mind over all the people she'd served this evening. No one had been drinking heavily, even the likely suspects, who were still chattering loudly from their table in the corner. Whatever it was, it couldn't have been drunk patrons. Still, it bothered her. Ten minutes later, when the cop hadn't returned, she tossed her apron on the counter and strode out. "Cover me for a couple minutes, Tui?"

"Sure thing, boss." Tui waved her away as she rang up a customer.

Katie stepped out into the cool night air. Red and blue lights flashed from a police cruiser in the car park. Two men looking thoroughly chastised slumped against the car while a constable in uniform wrote out what Katie assumed was a citation of some sort. Dale spoke in a low voice to one of the men and he shook his head.

The uniformed officer handed each man a slip of paper, and then waved them both away before turning to Dale. "Do you know the proprietor?" she asked.

"That would be me." Katie strode up and held a hand out to the woman. "Katie Cochrane. Thanks for coming out." Then she turned to Dale. "Sorry your meal was disrupted. It's on the house."

Dale held up a hand. "No. No worries. But seeing as I'm off duty and things here are sorted, I'll let Constable Daniels handle this from here." Dale returned to the restaurant.

"What happened?" Katie asked.

Constable Daniels referred to a notebook. "It seems a couple of your patrons left the bar and then got into a fight over" —she paused and shook her head— "melons."

"Excuse me?"

"Apparently, the merits of rock melon versus honeydew were enough to lead to a fist fight."

Katie laughed. "You're kidding."

"Miss Cochrane, it's clear these men were intoxicated. Their breath alcohol didn't register terribly high, but their behaviour ..." Her face was pained. "I'm going to have to write up the bar for serving intoxicated patrons."

*What?* "But I was at the bar all evening. I served those guys their drinks, and I can guarantee they each had no more than two beers. And before you say they must have preloaded, I know the law, and I pay attention to my customers. They weren't drunk."

"Their behaviour suggests otherwise."

Fair enough. Who gets into a fight over melons? Still, this was *her* bar. "They were *not* drunk. You said yourself that the breathalyser didn't show it, and I know I didn't serve them more than two beers each. Maybe they were just ... passionate about melons."

The policewoman stifled a laugh. "I'll take your statement into account. I'll have to report this, of course, but given the circumstances, maybe we can keep the bar out of it."

Katie let out a breath. "Thank you."

The woman smiled and nodded towards the building. "You've done a nice job with it. It was a bit of a pit before. I think the fire was the best thing that could have happened to it."

"Thanks. And thanks again for coming out." Katie shook Constable Daniels' hand, and the woman climbed into her cruiser and drove away.

# Chapter 8

## *A New Friend*

"Why are you at work already?"

Katie laughed. "The restaurant doesn't run itself, Aunt Rachael." She adjusted the volume of her earbuds so she could hear over the racket in the kitchen.

"What about your staff? Didn't you say you hired a baker?"

"She's a pastry chef, and she's great. But it's good for me to be here to help out."

Aunt Rachael huffed. "You work too hard."

"*You're* the one who bought me a pub. Maybe you should have thought about how much work owning a restaurant is before you made that decision, if you didn't want me to work hard."

"Working hard is one thing, but I can tell by your voice you're stressed out. If your staff is as good as you say they are, what has you tied in knots?"

Katie sighed. "It might be nothing, but the police were here two nights ago." She told her aunt about the fight in the car park, and how she might get written up for serving intoxicated customers.

"Well it sounds like you did nothing wrong, and in any case, there's nothing you can do about it, Katie. Get out of the kitchen and go for a walk."

"I can't just go for a walk; Jill needs me here."

"No I don't," Jill called from the other side of the kitchen. "A walk is a great idea."

Katie hoped Rachael hadn't heard that. No such luck.

"You see? I'm right. You work too hard, stress too much. Tell that baker of yours you'll be back later."

After a few more minutes of arguing, with Jill putting in her two cents now and again, Katie reluctantly closed the kitchen door behind her and stepped out into the cool morning air. She wasn't convinced that a walk would do her good—she wasn't into exercise, but Aunt Rachael would hound her next time they spoke, and the woman could sniff out a lie from ten kilometres away. Besides, Jill had promised to grill her when she returned to find out where she'd walked.

The only walking Katie had done in Rifton was between her rented house and the Tipsy Teapot. There didn't seem to be any time to explore more of the village. So as she left the restaurant, she turned the opposite direction from her house.

The footpath led her down a silent street lined with modest houses, most of which looked like they were built in the 1960s. She passed tidy gardens filled with roses, grassy fenced yards inhabited by yapping dogs, and mysterious sections surrounded by tall hedges. A large black cat sat on the top of a fence post watching her pass with unblinking yellow eyes.

Turning a corner, Katie was surprised to see a familiar face. Walking towards her was Alex Blackburn.

Alex smiled as she approached. "Morning Katie. I didn't know you walked."

Katie laughed. "I don't. Not usually. But my aunt insisted I get out for a walk this morning, because she claims I'm too stressed about work."

Alex nodded. "She's right, you know; walking is the perfect way to destress. I try to get out for a walk every day. Where were you heading?"

"I have no idea. I've never walked around Rifton."

"Come with me, then. I'll give you a tour." Alex led Katie on a circuitous tour filled with local history and gossip. They walked past the primary school and the Anglican church. "Apparently the church used to be the social centre of the community," Alex said. "But now there are only services there once a fortnight."

They walked through the cemetery, which creeped Katie out a little, but Alex seemed at home among the graves. She stopped at one with a crisp granite stone that read, *Alice Taylor nee Smithson, 1935–2022, Queen of Compost.* Carved below the writing was a spade. "My grandmother," Alex said simply.

"I remember you said she was in the gardening group, right?"

"Yeah. Has the group been into the restaurant yet?"

"Yes." Katie laughed. "They brought me gifts when I opened."

"Don't tell me—Jane gave you worm wee."

"How did you know?"

"She brings me a bottle every two weeks, for Gran's— my—garden. The women insist I keep the garden up."

They walked on through the cemetery, and Alex pointed out various graves, with anecdotes about the people. Here was the man Alex's grandmother had an affair with. There was Shelby's great-great-grandmother, Catherine Parker. And there were Mary and Clive Saunders, Shelby's great-grandparents and former owners of the Rifton Pub. Finally, they passed a small plot of rank grass enclosed by a rusted chain fence.

"And here is Shelby's great-great-great-grandmother."

"There's no stone," Katie commented.

Alex shook her head. "She was supposedly a witch, and apparently her own son-in-law started the house fire that killed her."

"Wow!" Katie shook her head. "I had no idea there was so much sordid history in Rifton."

"Yep. Some interesting stuff has happened here. Of course, if you're looking for a nightlife or anything, you're out of luck."

"Ha! Like I have any time for recreational activities. Besides, I spend every day in a bar; why would I want to go out to one?"

"Fair enough."

They continued their walk, chatting about Rifton, themselves, Katie's plans for the pub. By the time they circled back to the Tipsy Teapot, Katie's tension had evaporated. "Thanks for the tour," she said to Alex.

"Thanks for joining me. You know, I walk every day before work. You're welcome to join me."

Katie didn't have to consider it for long. She might not be into exercise, but the walk had left her refreshed, and she really liked Alex. It had been so long since she'd spent time with someone who wasn't in the restaurant business, she'd forgotten how nice it was to talk about things other than the latest irate customer debacle, or how the head chef was a dick. "I'd love to. This has been exactly what I needed." They exchanged numbers and set a time to meet up the following morning.

Before they said goodbye, Alex tipped her head to the side, squinting at something over Katie's shoulder. "Those plants," she said, and Katie turned.

"The ones with the red flowers?" Katie asked. "Yeah, I

have no idea what they are. The women from the garden group asked about them too."

"But have you transplanted them? Because I was sure they were further from the road on Saturday night."

"No. I haven't done anything with them."

Alex shrugged. "Well, I *did* have a couple of beers that night. I might not have been paying much attention." She said goodbye and headed down the street.

Katie frowned at the odd plants. Were they closer to the road than they had been the other day?

Of course not. Plants couldn't move. She wasn't much of a gardener, but she did know plants had roots.

She turned and stepped into the kitchen to start her day for the second time, feeling much more relaxed this time around.

# Interlude 3

## *1960*

Sean Fraser unlocked the back door to the Rifton Pub and heaved four bags of groceries onto the bench by the door. He passed through the silent kitchen, flicking the oven to a warming setting on his way through. He turned on the lights in the main room, and then unlocked the front door, turning the sign to *open*.

His first customers weren't likely to show up for at least half an hour, giving Sean time to prepare. He returned to the kitchen, extracting a foil-wrapped tray of pies from the refrigerator and sliding them into the warming oven. His baker, Sally, made them on Monday, Wednesday and Friday. Sean reckoned she could probably bake just once a week—no one cared what the pies tasted like, whether they were a day old or five days old didn't matter. But it was easier for Sally to make smaller batches around her kids' school schedule.

With the pies warming up, Sean jogged up the creaky steps to his flat. Well, he called it his flat. It was technically just two rooms of the hotel he'd reserved for his own use—a bedroom and a sitting room. He rarely had overnight guests, and it made life easy to live above the bar.

He shrugged off his coat and hat, and then walked to the other side of the building and poked his head into Room Four, one of the rooms he rented out occasionally, where he knew he'd find Thunder. "Hey fleabag. I brought some fish heads for you."

The sleek grey cat curled up on the bed raised his head, yawned and stretched.

Sean knew the cat was trying to look nonchalant, but also knew he would follow him back downstairs.

Thunder had been old Mary Saunders' cat. He apparently never got the message that she sold the pub, and even before she passed away, he was often found hanging out there. Now that she was gone, he'd moved in full-time.

Sean didn't mind—not that he thought he could do anything about it if he did. The cat seemed to be able to sneak in and out of the pub like smoke. But he kept the rats in check, and it was nice to have a companion after hours, even if the cat was aloof much of the time.

In the kitchen, Sean dropped two odiferous fish heads into Thunder's food dish. The cat pounced on them instantly, crunching the bones in his back teeth and making a sound halfway between a purr and a growl.

While the cat ate, Sean unloaded his groceries. Most were for personal use, but Sally had given him a list of ingredients she needed for next week's pies—items that were cheaper to pick up in town.

The front door opened and banged shut. Sean stepped out to greet his first customer. "Nate," he greeted the regular. "The usual?"

"Yes please." Nate settled onto a stool and lit a cigarette.

"You're late today." Sean pulled the man a pint of beer and set it on the counter.

Nate blew out a cloud of smoke. "Yeah. Milking machine broke. Spent half the morning repairing it."

"Steak and onion, or pork?"

"Steak today. Thanks." Nate was a daily customer. His early morning shift at the Davis family's dairy farm ended at half past twelve, and the Rifton Pub was his lunch stop.

Two more lunch customers wandered in while Nate was eating. At one-thirty, the guys from the local cheese factory showed up. Sean could practically set his watch by his locals.

Around four o'clock, a stranger stepped in. By the time he reached the bar, Thunder was at his feet, sniffing his ankles.

Hmm. Would the man ask for Room Four?

The man was lanky and tall. Otherwise, he was completely unremarkable. They all were, these strangers. Sean greeted the man as he approached. "Afternoon, sir. What can I get you?"

"I'm looking for a room for the night."

Thunder leapt to the bar and sat facing the man, tail tip twitching.

"Is Room Four available?"

Nailed it. Sean stole a glance at the cat. How did the animal know? And what was up with Room Four anyway? Thunder insisted on hanging out there, and if the cat took an interest in a customer, they invariably asked specifically for the room. It made no sense.

But Sean wasn't going to turn down custom, even if it was uncanny. "It is. Just the one night?"

The man nodded. Sean took his money and handed

him the key. "Up the stairs and to the left. Bathroom is at the top of the stairs." Thunder slunk along behind as the man mounted the stairs. Sean hoped the cat hadn't left too much fur on the duvet.

The after-work rush started a short while later, and the hour from five to closing time was a blur. As usual, there was a group of guys who pushed their luck at the end of the day.

"Come on. Just one more round. What's another fifteen minutes?" asked the owner of the local petrol station, a regular who practically guzzled his beer every time, because he didn't arrive until after five-thirty.

Sean shook his head. "I agree, but I'm not going to risk my liquor licence because you want another beer."

"Weren't you lobbying for longer hours?" he asked.

"Yeah. It's ridiculous to have to close at six. But tell that to the politicians who want to look all righteous for voters." It was a sore point for Sean. The pub barely broke even some months, and another hour or two of sales in the evening would make a huge difference. But he knew how closely some of the local council members watched him—waiting for him to breach his licence so they could take it away. He wasn't going to push his luck.

He bundled his last customers out the door at six on the dot, turned the sign to *closed*, and locked the door. He slid the last of the glasses into the dishwasher and turned it on, then swept and mopped the floor and wiped down the bar. He slipped the last remaining pie onto a plate, pulled himself a beer, and headed upstairs.

Something thumped on the floor in Room Four. The man had never come down for dinner, had he? Sean briefly thought about knocking on the door and offering him the pie he carried. But if the man had wanted dinner, he'd have come down.

At the top of the stairs, Sean heard a voice muttering. Who was the guy talking to? He snorted a laugh. Probably to the damn cat, who no doubt had snuck into the room with him. Sean turned to the right and headed to his sitting room to enjoy his pie.

Late that night, Sean woke suddenly. Had that been an earthquake? Maybe it was just the train, although it rarely woke him anymore. He lay in bed listening. A thump sounded, then the yowl of a cat.

"What the hell?" Sean threw the covers back and pulled on a pair of pants. He stepped into the hallway and listened. Scuffling sounds emanated from Room Four, then another yowl. What was going on? He strode to Room Four and knocked on the door. "Everything okay in there?"

More scuffling, a grunt, and a snapping sound. "Yes, fine, thanks," called the man. His voice sounded strained.

"You sure you don't need anything?"

Something scraped along the floor, and then the door opened. The man was breathing hard, his hair dishevelled and his shirt untucked. "I'm fine. Thanks. Um ... any chance of breakfast in the morning?"

"No. Sorry." Sean tried to peek around the man to see what was going on. Did he have a woman up here? How would he have gotten her in?

"No worries. Goodnight." The door clicked shut.

Sean stood in the hallway for a moment longer. All was silent inside Room Four. Then he shook his head and returned to his room.

He didn't bother with the light, but kicked his pants off and slipped back into bed. When his legs hit a warm furry body, he jerked back. "What the hell are you doing in my bed?" Hadn't he just heard the cat in Room Four?

Thunder hissed.

"Hey, it's *my* bed, mate." He shook the covers, and the cat shot out from under them and leapt to the floor. Sean settled himself and shut his eyes. A minute later, the cat jumped back onto the bed and curled himself on top of the duvet next to Sean's side.

"Bloody cat," he mumbled, before falling back to sleep.

# Chapter 9

## *Dinner Date*

Alex wasn't much of a cook. "Why did I suggest this?" she asked in a panic as she pulled the lasagne out of a smoking oven.

Shel leaned over her shoulder. "It looks and smells great. It's just the stuff that spilled onto the oven floor that's smoking."

"But Katie is a *chef*!" Why did she think she could cook for someone who was a professional at it?

A knock sounded on the door.

"Shit!" Alex said, surveying the disaster area that was her kitchen.

"Relax," Shel said. "I'll get the door."

Alex set the lasagne on a cooling rack and frantically began tossing dirty dishes into the sink and wiping down the bench.

"Oh my god! That smells amazing!" Katie entered and stepped over to where the lasagne sat. She inhaled deeply. "Tell me you made garlic bread, too."

"I did, though I can't imagine it's as good as what you can make."

"Are you kidding?" Katie said. "This looks and smells great. No one *ever* cooks for me. This is an incredible treat." She set an insulated bag on the kitchen bench and pulled out a bottle of wine. "I hope you drink red."

Alex answered by pulling out three glasses and setting them down. "Yes, please." Her nerves were only slightly calmed by Katie's enthusiastic entrance.

"If you'll put this into the freezer, I'll pour," Katie said, withdrawing a carton of ice cream from the bag.

Shel stepped forward and took the ice cream. "Oh yeah. Boysenberry. The *best*."

"Whew!" Katie said. "I was worried you guys might be more triple chocolate types."

Alex laughed. "Oh, I like triple chocolate, too. If it's ice cream, I'm all over it."

"Me too," Shel agreed.

Alex passed out the wine and raised her glass. "Cheers."

"Cheers," Katie and Shel replied.

Katie took a sip, and then jerked her glass away from her mouth to look down. "Oh! Who are you?"

Thor twined around Katie's legs, his long black tail twisting around her ankles. He rubbed his face against her shoe.

"He's a friendly thing." Katie bent to scratch his ears.

Alex and Shelby shared a wide-eyed look. Thor didn't take to just anyone. He had minimal use for most people. He'd latched onto Shelby, though. Alex was convinced it was because Shelby was the descendant of a witch. Did his interest in Katie mean she was, too?

"So, Katie. Tell me a little about yourself," Shel said. "Alex says you're from Timaru."

"Yeah." Katie gave Thor a final pat and stood.

"And how was Timaru as a place to grow up?"

Katie shrugged. "Well, you know Timaru—it's not a big place. We kids hung out in front of the local dairy, eating ice creams. Walked down to the beach in the summer. That was about the extent of the excitement."

Shel smiled. "Well that sounds better than growing up in Rifton. Timaru's practically the big smoke by comparison."

"I don't know. Alex took me on a tour of the cemetery— sounds like there's been a lot of excitement here in the past. Most of it within your family?"

Well, that was a convenient turn of the conversation. Alex hoped Shel would take advantage of it. If he didn't, she would.

"Yeah, my family's been in Rifton for a long time, and there were some real characters. I think more than one of my ancestors dabbled in witchcraft."

"What about you?" Alex asked Katie. "Got any crazy witches in your family?"

Katie shook her head. "No—but my Aunt Rachael *is* crazy. Who buys their niece a burnt-out pub for her birthday?"

"True." Alex carried the lasagne to the table. "How's it been going? Are you happy with how much business you're getting?"

"It's been great. I want to start holding events—quiz nights, theme nights, happy hours, special deals—to try to fill in the times that are slow, but it's done better than I expected, actually."

They sat down, and Alex served up the lasagne and passed around the basket of garlic bread. She waited nervously while Katie took her first bite.

"Mmm. That's fabulous, Alex. Thank you for cooking."

"Whew!" Alex finally relaxed. "I can't tell you how terrifying it was to cook for you."

"I love when people cook for me. Mum's practically the only one who will do it anymore, though."

"So do you like owning your own place, rather than working for someone else?" Shelby asked.

Katie laughed. "Most of the time, but I don't think I realised just how much shit the owner has to deal with. I'd hoped to be in the kitchen a whole lot more, but instead I'm dealing with staff scheduling, bills, purchasing, payroll ... Not that I didn't know those were part of it, but I didn't count on how much of my time they'd take up. And to top it all off, this week I've been dealing with the police."

"The police! What happened?" Alex asked.

"A pair of guys left the bar on Saturday night and got into a fist fight in the car park. Someone rang the cops, and before I knew it, they were talking about citing me for serving intoxicated people."

"Oh no! Had the men been drinking a lot?"

"That's just it—they'd had two beers each. I know, because I was bartending Saturday night. Even the policewoman said their breath alcohol level wasn't super high."

"But they were going to cite you for it? How does that work?"

Katie rolled her eyes. "I know, right? They didn't end up citing me, but it took half my week to sort it all out."

"Well, hopefully it won't be a regular occurrence," Shel said.

"Let's hope not."

After dinner, Alex made tea, and they took their mugs out to the back deck, where they could relax in the deckchairs.

"Wow! You weren't kidding," Katie said. "Your grandmother was quite the gardener. This is beautiful."

"Yeah. I try to keep it weeded, and I planted a few vegetables in the veggie patch, but it was so much better kept up when she was alive." Alex sipped her tea and wondered if the garden group would be willing to pop in and give her some pointers someday.

"Did she have a big dog?" Katie nodded towards the large chain-link cage filling half the lawn.

Alex glanced at Shel, and he gave a little head shake. Yeah. Katie didn't need to know the truth, that the cage had housed the large demonic centipede Alex had accidentally summoned. "Parrots," she lied.

"Really? What kind?"

Shit. Alex scrambled to remember a type of parrot. "Sulphur-crested cockatoos."

Thor strolled around the corner of the house and onto the deck. He made a beeline for Katie, jumping onto her lap.

"She had birds and cats?" Katie asked, pushing Thor's tail out of her face. "Seems like a bad combination." Thor sniffed Katie's mug, and then leapt to the deck.

Alex shrugged. "They mostly ignored each other."

"And you kept the cat, but not the birds?"

Okay, this was getting awkward, talking about her gran's parrots that never existed. "Yeah, the birds were noisy and a lot of work."

Shel came to her rescue, asking Katie, "Do you have any pets?" Thor jumped to his lap and curled up, eyes on Katie, as though he was awaiting her answer.

Katie shook her head. "I've always rented places that don't allow them." She sounded wistful.

"Did you have pets growing up?" Alex asked.

"No, but Aunt Rachael has always had cats—lots of them—and I loved visiting her and playing with the kittens."

"Ah, so she's not only crazy, she's a crazy cat lady?" Shel's eyes flicked to Alex's for a moment.

Katie laughed. "Yeah, that about sums her up."

Alex thought there was probably more to Aunt Rachael than Katie knew.

# Chapter 10

## *Strike Two*

Another Saturday night at the pub, and Katie was down a staff member again. This time it was her dishwasher, Karl. His daughter had broken her leg on a bouncy castle an hour before his shift started, so he was sitting in the urgent care clinic posting updates on social media while Katie helped cover his duties.

Steam billowed from the dishwasher as she raised the door and slid a warm tray of clean glasses out. She hefted the tray and carried it out to the bar. As she pulled the glasses out and stacked them under the bar, Tui leaned close to her.

"Hot surly dude's here again. I dare you to get his name," she whispered.

Katie rolled her eyes and didn't reply. Short staffed on a Saturday night, she wasn't going to waste time harassing a customer, but she did glance up. Just like last week, the man was dressed as if for work, and looking slightly windblown. He sat down at the bar not far from where Katie was working, and Taine greeted him.

"What can I get you?" Taine asked.

The man glanced at Katie, then back at Taine before ordering the same beer he'd drunk last week. Katie finished emptying her tray and returned to the kitchen to grab the next one. When she returned, Taine and Tui had their heads together in whispered conversation. Tui smiled as they broke apart. Was something going on between them? Tui was supposedly dating one of the line cooks at Brennan's, but it wouldn't be the first time she'd been double dipping.

Although Katie tried to ignore the man at the bar, she couldn't help noticing he once again looked morosely into his beer, as though he didn't really want to be here. Why would you go drink expensive beer in a bar if you weren't going to enjoy it?

As she unloaded glasses, Taine came to help. "Can you watch the bar for me while I have my break?" he asked.

"Is it that late already?" It always surprised Katie how fast some nights went by. "Yeah, sure." She set the last two glasses on the shelf.

"I'll take the tray back on my way out." Taine took it from Katie and headed to the kitchen. He gave Tui a nudge as he passed. Definitely something up between those two.

Katie didn't have time to dwell on the possible budding romance between two of her employees; the restaurant was busy, and she spent a solid half hour serving drinks.

When she had a moment, she approached 'hot surly dude'. "Everything okay here? Can I get you something to eat?"

He raised his eyes from his beer, and a ghost of a smile flitted across his face. "No thanks." He lowered his head again.

Okay. At least he didn't frown at her. "Well, just sing out if you need a refill or anything." She looked at the time. Where was Taine? His break was over a while ago.

"He's taken over the dishwashing. Figured you'd appreciate the break," Tui said when Katie asked.

"Oh, that's nice of him. Yeah, I do appreciate the break." It's not that she minded dishwashing that much, but the monotony of it got to her after a while. She'd get stuck in her own head and start stressing about all the other things she had to do. On the customer-facing jobs, she was too busy interacting with people to stress out about other things.

"So, hot surly dude can't keep his eyes off you," Tui whispered.

"What? He barely glanced at me when I asked him if he wanted anything else."

Tui smirked. "Yeah, but whenever *you're* not looking at *him*, *he's* looking at *you*. I think he was disappointed you weren't tending bar when he arrived. That's why Taine went for his break early—to get you behind the bar."

"What? I thought it was too early for his break. We're too busy for you two to be playing games." Katie broke away from Tui and plastered on a smile as a customer approached. She served a few drinks, and then leaned towards Tui again and hissed, "What's he doing now?"

Tui frowned. "Leaving."

Katie turned. Sure enough, hot surly dude's glass was empty and he was standing to go. Katie was inexplicably disappointed—he wasn't a particularly good customer, nursing one beer for an hour—she should be happy he was leaving and freeing up space for bigger spenders. He glanced up, gave a brief smile and a nod, then left.

A moment later, Kelli, one of her line cooks burst through the kitchen door. "Katie? We have a situation."

Shit. Katie slipped into the kitchen and followed as Kelli strode to the back, filling her in.

"I was on my break," Kelli began, "and this woman in the car park climbed onto the top of an SUV and started singing and dancing."

"Shit. Did someone ring the police?" Katie did *not* need another run-in with the cops.

"I don't think so. There was no one else in the car park except the woman and the guy she was with. I tried to get her to come down, but the guy kept egging her on."

"Come on. Maybe between the two of us we can deal with this before someone involves the police." Katie and Kelli pushed their way out the back door and hurried into the car park.

"Oh my god! My leg!" A woman's panicked voice rang out, and Katie broke into a run towards a huddle of three people next to a white SUV.

A woman lay on the ground, her leg bent at a horribly unnatural angle. A man knelt at her side, hands on her shoulders. "Stay still. You've hit your head too."

The third person was hot surly dude. He had his phone to his ear. "Yeah. Fell off the roof of a car—definitely a broken leg, also hit her head ... yes ... no. Great. Thanks." He pulled the phone away from his ear. "Ambulance is on its way."

"What happened here?" Katie asked, though she hardly needed to—it was obvious.

"Well, I'm not sure what she was doing on the roof of the car, but I was coming out to my vehicle, and I saw her fall off," hot surly dude replied.

The man on the ground spoke up, his voice shaking and edged with panic. "She was singing. It's my fault. I suggested it. But it was a joke—I didn't think she'd actually do it."

The woman on the ground moaned.

"You've called emergency services?" Katie asked hot surly dude.

He nodded. "They said they'd be here soon, and not to move her."

Katie turned to Kelli. "You can probably go back inside. Tell Taine to get back to the bar. I'll wait for the ambulance." Her stomach clenched. How much had this woman had to drink? She tried to remember, but she had no idea. The woman had been sitting at a table in the dining room, and Katie didn't know how many of the drinks she'd fixed had gone to that table. Quentin or Molly would know.

The faint sound of a siren began to grow in the distance. Before long, the ambulance was turning into the car park, lights flashing.

The paramedics were efficient. As they examined the woman and got her onto a stretcher, they questioned the men who'd seen what happened. They bundled her into the ambulance. The woman's companion jumped into his car and followed as the ambulance pulled out.

Hot surly dude turned to go, but Katie put a hand on his arm. "Thank you for helping out. I hate to ask, but since you witnessed what happened, I'd like to get your name and number, just in case the police get involved."

"Why would the police get involved? She was being an idiot and had an accident."

Katie sighed. "If she was drunk, my restaurant could be cited for serving an intoxicated person."

"*Your* restaurant? I thought you were the bartender."

Katie laughed. "I sometimes have to fill in for my employees."

"You *own* the Tipsy Teapot?" The man's voice held a note of incredulity that irritated Katie.

"Yes, which is why I'd like to make sure I have contact information for the only witness to what happened here this evening." Katie pulled out the notebook and pen she always carried in her apron pocket—she was forever writing down notes to herself. Order more serviettes, find a new mushroom supplier, call the plumber about the leaky faucet in the women's loo ... if she didn't write them down, she'd forget to do them when the next emergency came up.

"Oh. Yeah. Of course." Hot surly dude took the notebook and pen, and scrawled his name and number on it. He smiled as he handed it back to her.

She glanced down at the page. Finn Laird. "Thanks Finn. Hopefully I won't need to ring you."

"No worries." Finn opened his mouth as if to say something more, then closed it again. He nodded and smiled, then walked to his car.

Katie returned to the kitchen to find her employees frantic, dirty dishes piled high on the bench. She dove into the pile, rinsing plates and shoving them into the dishwasher as quickly as she could.

When Katie finally locked the doors for the night, she was exhausted. She *so* needed to hire a couple of casual staff. She'd posted the job ad earlier in the week, but only had one applicant so far. Unfortunately, Katie had worked with the woman before, and knew she was a drama queen. Katie wouldn't hire her unless she was desperate.

After tonight, she was almost ready to hire anyone. She mounted the stairs to her office to put the cash in the safe. It was only ten-thirty—if she did a little bit of work this evening, maybe she could sleep in for half an hour in the morning. She collapsed into her desk chair and pulled out her notebook.

She paged through today's scribbles. Some things couldn't be dealt with at this hour, but if she did this week's online ordering now, it would take some stress off her day tomorrow.

She flipped the page, and there was Finn's name and number. "Finn Laird." It was a good name. It suited his look.

Katie laughed. She'd have to tell Tui tomorrow that she'd not only gotten his name, but also his number.

Not that she was going to contact him unless she had to. Tui might still view Katie as the fun-loving, carefree university student she used to be, but she was different now.

No. She wasn't different—she'd still love nothing more than to spend Saturday nights dancing, to pick up cute guys, to party until the wee hours of the morning—it was her responsibilities that had changed. She didn't have time to go dancing or pick up guys. She was too exhausted to stay up later than absolutely necessary.

Is this what turning thirty did to you? Made you feel ... old? Made you act like an adult?

*No, this is what owning a restaurant does,* she reminded herself. And in spite of her exhaustion and stress, she *loved* owning her own place. Every time she arrived at work, she looked up at the building and grinned. This was hers, and she would put into it whatever it took. If that meant no dancing, no dates, that was okay. Maybe once she had a few extra staff she'd be able to relax more.

Katie shut her notebook and opened her laptop. The sooner she got this ordering finished, the sooner she could go home.

It took only twenty minutes to send off her order. Her fingers hovered over the keyboard for a moment, her mind still on Finn Laird. She wouldn't ring him, but she *could* find out more about him. Before she could think too much about it, she typed his name into the search engine.

Hmm. He was on LinkedIn and Facebook. She clicked on his Facebook profile. That was more likely to tell her what she wanted to know. Namely, whether the guy was single.

"Aw, come on, Finn. Fill out your Facebook profile," Katie muttered as she scanned the blank fields for relationships, school, places, and workplaces.

There were a few photos: Finn astride a mountain bike with a rocky peak behind him, Finn on his knees beside two goofy-looking chocolate labs, Finn and an older man standing in front of the sign for Beefy Bernard's Bar and Grill, Finn cheek to cheek with a blonde woman at the beach.

Damn. Girlfriend? There was no way to know. By looks, she could have been his sister. Katie clicked on Finn's friends list and scrolled through, looking for the same woman. She wasn't there. But the older guy was—Bernard Fischer. She clicked onto his profile.

Bernard had posted the same photo of himself and Finn in front of the restaurant sign. *My nephew has moved to Darfield!* Nephew, eh?

Bernard's profile was full of photos of a restaurant, but in Katie's exhausted state it took her a few minutes to connect the dots. Finn's uncle was the owner of Beefy Bernard's Bar and Grill in Darfield. Fascinating, but Katie was more interested in who the woman was. No point in even thinking about Finn unless he was single.

Katie yawned and closed her laptop. It was time to go home and get some sleep.

# Chapter 11

## *Fighting Flowers*

A knock sounded at Alex's door at seven o'clock Wednesday evening. She and Shel were doing the dishes, and they both looked up and frowned.

"Who could that be?" Shel asked.

Alex sighed. "Probably Linda." Alex's next-door neighbour was kind, but nosey. "She probably wants to check if you're here." Shelby all but lived at Alex's place now. He'd upgraded her internet service and bought her a new router to improve her Wi-Fi so he could work from her place. He'd moved his computer set-up to her spare bedroom. Said it was a much quieter space to work than his bedroom in his parents' place, now that his dad had officially retired. Most weekdays, he showed up before Alex left for work. They enjoyed a coffee together before they went their separate ways for the day. When Alex got home, they made dinner together. Some nights, he never made it back to his parents' house. No doubt Linda suspected as much and wanted to confirm her suspicions so she could gossip about them.

Alex dried her hands and went to answer the door.

"Hi Alex!" It wasn't Linda, but Jane Walker, along with all the other members of the garden group. "We hate to barge in like this, but ... well, there's something I think we need to discuss with you. Do you still have that book from your gran?"

Oh no. This wasn't good. *That book* Jane referred to was *Formulae for the Summoning of Minor Angels and Daemons*, a strange and ancient book that had caused Alex all manner of trouble since she discovered it among Gran's possessions. "Come on in. I'll put on the kettle." Alex opened the door wide and greeted all five of the women as they entered.

"Oh good! Shelby's here too," Ellen said. She squeezed Alex's arm and whispered, "I hope he's staying the night."

Alex stifled a laugh and pulled out a box of tea. "I'm afraid I only have gumboot." She'd tossed all of Gran's herbal teas. They all tasted like grass to her.

"No worries. We've brought our own." The women drew various boxes of tea from their bags, along with three tins of cookies.

Shel leaned close to her and muttered, "It was premeditated, whatever this is." He pulled out seven mugs from the cupboard and set them on the bench as the kettle came to a boil.

When they all had tea and were seated in the living room, Alex's curiosity couldn't be contained anymore. "So, what's this about?"

Jane drew herself up. "Well, we were at the Tipsy Teapot yesterday for morning tea."

"I had the most amazing cinnamon scroll," interrupted Ellen. "I think it was even better than Mansfield Bakery."

"And there's still something not quite right about Katie's carrot cake frosting, but I do recommend it," Sharon added.

Jane gave Ellen and Sharon a withering look and continued. "We noticed on our way in that those bushes with the red flowers in the car park have spread. So we asked Katie about them again. She couldn't tell us what they were."

"So I asked if we could take cuttings," Pauline said.

Sharon shook her head. "You *know* they won't grow if you get permission to take them. They've got to be stolen."

"Well it didn't matter in the end," Margaret said, "because we couldn't take a cutting."

"Did you go back later with secateurs?" Shelby asked.

Pauline laughed. "No, we had secateurs—I carry them in my purse at all times."

"We couldn't get a cutting because the plants *fought back*!" Margaret's eyes sparkled with excitement.

Alex frowned. "What do you mean, they fought back?"

"The branches were like iron," Pauline said. "And as I was struggling to snip one off, another branch reached around and bit me." She held out her bandaged hand.

Shelby turned to Alex. "I *told* you it bit."

Alex shook her head. "Plants don't bite. I mean, I know about Venus fly traps, but ..." she blanched. "Are you saying ..."

Margaret nodded. "We think they're not actually plants."

Alex's stomach clenched. "And you want to see if they're in Gran's book." Hell. Why did they have to drag her into this? She stood to retrieve the book. As she walked down the hallway, she passed Thor trotting in the other direction.

When she returned to the living room with the leather-bound book in hand, Thor was inspecting all the women, sniffing their ankles, jumping to the backs of their chairs to peer at them. They all greeted him warmly—they knew what he was. They'd been there when Gran had summoned him.

Alex handed the book to Jane. "I don't remember any demon in there that looked like a plant."

The women all crowded around to look as Jane slowly paged through the book, scanning picture after picture of bizarre creatures. The demons had feathers, fur, claws, tails, wings, and sharp teeth, but no leaves or flowers.

"Are you sure the plant bit you?" Alex asked. "Maybe the wind blew the branch towards your hand. They have thorns."

Pauline shook her head. "It *held on*."

"I had to give it a whack with my purse to get it to let go," Margaret said.

Thor jumped to Pauline's lap and sniffed at her bandaged hand. He growled. Conversation stopped, and all eyes were on the cat as he licked Pauline's hand and nipped at the bandage.

"Take off the bandage," Shel said.

"What? And let a demonic cat lick an open wound?" Pauline looked horrified.

Shel nodded. "Trust me. Is the wound bothersome?"

"Yes, it itches terribly, but—"

"You know what Thor is. He did this when Alex was bitten by the materpoda." The giant demonic centipede Alex had accidentally summoned a few months ago. "His saliva healed her arm."

"You let him lick it?" Pauline wrinkled her nose.

"If you don't, he'll" —Thor sank his teeth into Pauline's hand, and she yelped— "bite you."

"Just take the bandage off," Margaret said.

"You're kidding. The beast bit me!" Pauline cradled her injured hand against her chest while Thor growled at her.

"Shel's right, Pauline." Alex tried to make her voice as soothing as possible. "It will be fine. Let Thor lick the wound."

Reluctantly, Pauline peeled the bandage off her hand and held it out to Thor. The cat pounced on it, making Pauline flinch, but he didn't bite or claw, only lapped at the bite he'd inflicted, and then at the inflamed skin around the wound the plant had made.

Pauline sucked in a breath, and Ellen exclaimed, "Oh. My. God."

"Well look at that," Sharon said.

Thor pulled away from Pauline and leapt to the floor. He sat on his haunches and washed a paw. Alex thought he looked inordinately pleased with himself. The show-off.

Pauline raised her hand and inspected it. "The marks are gone—all of them."

"I wonder if my Leo can do that," Margaret said.

"That's right." Alex turned to Margaret. "I forgot you had a demonic cat too."

"Please, I prefer to think of him as a familiar, not a demon."

"Right. A familiar. So Leo has never done anything like this?"

Margaret shook her head. "I'll have to ask him about it."

"Could you ask him about the plants at the Tipsy Teapot?" Shel asked. "Maybe he knows what they are."

Margaret snorted. "I can ask. Whether he'll deign to tell me what he knows is the question."

"Isn't a familiar sort of like your servant or something? Doesn't he have to do your bidding?" Shel asked.

This got a full-fledged laugh from Margaret. "Not Leo. He claims I summoned him for one purpose—to look after my mother—and that anything additional he does for me is a bonus, and I should be grateful for it." She leaned forward and whispered conspiratorially, "He likes to act as though he doesn't care, but I think he secretly enjoys being helpful."

"Well, if you can ask him what he knows, that would be great," Alex said. "Is there anywhere else we could go for information about the plants?" She looked around the room at the women. "Any of you have any more books on summoning?"

The women all shook their heads. Margaret pursed her lips. "I have a friend in Hamilton who dabbles in witchcraft. I can ask her."

Shel met Alex's gaze. "We could do some online searching."

Alex nodded. "If we can verify that these plants are actually demons and find the summoning spell, we should be able to perform the banishment and get rid of them." They *would* need to get rid of them. Plants that bit people? It wasn't exactly the sort of pest you wanted running rampant anywhere, and especially not in the car park of a restaurant.

"Do you think we should tell Katie?" Shel asked.

Alex shook her head. "No. The poor woman is stressed enough. And do you think she'd believe us if we told her she had demonic plants growing at the pub?"

"Fair enough."

"Well, we should get going." Jane stood, and the other women followed suit, gathering their teabags and biscuit tins.

"Let us know if you learn anything," Shel said.

"You too," Margaret replied.

Ellen squeezed Alex's arm on the way out and whispered, "Don't do anything I wouldn't do. Have a nice night." She winked and then looked pointedly at Shel.

Alex rolled her eyes and shut the door behind them.

# Interlude 4

## *1993*

Simon Harris yawned and scratched his unshaved chin. He hated when they had overnight guests at the pub. The combination of late nights at the pub and early opening for the hotel guests was exhausting. Good thing it didn't happen often. Maybe he should suggest to Liz that they close the accommodation. Now that the fine for running a pub without providing accommodation had been lifted, it was hardly worth keeping the rooms up. Maybe they could even fix up the upstairs as a flat and move in, saving on the rent they currently paid for a house.

He flicked on the lights in the bar and made himself a cup of coffee on the expensive espresso machine Liz had insisted they purchase. He wasn't certain it had been worth the expense, but he had to admit it made a damn good cuppa. Upstairs, their guest was thumping around in her room.

Thunder, the sleek grey cat that had come with the pub when Simon and Liz had purchased it, leapt to the bar.

"Get off, beast. You know you're not supposed to be there." Simon waved a hand at the cat. The animal ignored him, sauntering the length of the bar before dropping to the floor and padding to his food dish in the kitchen.

Simon sipped his coffee while he made a list of items he needed to pick up in town. The repairs to the pub never seemed to end—as soon as he fixed one thing, something else broke. Last week it was a flooded toilet in the men's room, this week a faulty thermostat on the deep fat fryer. Simon was handy with repairs, but every job seemed to require three trips to town for the necessary parts.

More thumping upstairs, and then the bang of the door to Room Four signalled that their guest—an older woman named Mrs Hettrick—was on her way down for breakfast or to check out. Simon hoped it was the latter—the sooner he made the trip to town, the sooner he could get the fryer back up and running. What was a pub that couldn't serve fish and chips?

Mrs Hettrick's suitcase thumped down the steps, and Simon jumped up to help her. "Here, let me get that bag for you," he said as he mounted the stairs, meeting her halfway.

"Oh. Thank you." She flashed him a smile and relinquished her hold on the handle.

"Will you be having breakfast, Mrs. Hettrick?" Damn, her suitcase was heavy. He didn't remember it being this much of a struggle when he'd lugged it up the stairs for her yesterday afternoon. But then, his coffee hadn't kicked in yet this morning

"Just a flat white, I think," she replied. "To take away."

Mrs Hettrick rummaged in her purse as she approached the bar. Simon parked her suitcase beside her and circled around the bar. He fixed her coffee and took payment, then lugged her bag to her car.

As Mrs Hettrick drove away, Liz pulled into the car park, backing into the loading area for deliveries. Simon gave her a peck on the cheek as she stepped out of the car. "All done?"

"All fresh and clean," said his wife with a smile. She'd spent the night washing all the restaurant's linens after a mouse had gotten into the cupboard and soiled them.

Simon hefted the heavy basket of linens out of the boot and carried it inside, Liz on his heels. He helped her stow the linens in the cupboard, which he'd cleaned after patching the mouse hole in the rear corner. Then he headed to town for the fryer parts he needed.

Four hours later, when Simon returned, he found Liz in the kitchen sipping a glass of wine and looking pale.

"Liz?" His wife rarely drank, and never before lunch on a Tuesday. "What's wrong?"

"I went upstairs to strip the bed in Room Four." The wine sloshed as her hand shook. "There were ... bugs ... in the room. Big ones."

"Bugs?" Liz wasn't fond of spiders, but Simon had never seen her this shaken by creepy crawlies. "You mean, like, bed bugs? Spiders?"

His wife shuddered. "I don't know. They were horrible! I ... I just ran out and slammed the door shut."

"Well, I'll go up and take a l—"

"No!" Liz clutched his arm. "Don't open the door."

Wow. He'd never seen Liz like this before. He gave

her hand a reassuring squeeze. "Honey, it's okay. They're just bugs. Do you want me to ring an exterminator? We can leave the room shut until the exterminator has been through. If we get any overnight guests, we can put them in one of the other rooms."

Liz nodded. "I think that would be best."

The exterminator couldn't make it to the pub until Friday, and Liz was so jumpy and on edge by Thursday afternoon, that Simon suggested she visit her sister and return on Saturday, once the infestation had been dealt with.

"Promise me you won't open that door until the exterminator is here," she implored.

Simon resisted the frown he felt growing— something was wrong with his wife and he didn't like it. Instead, he gave her a reassuring nod and a firm embrace. "I won't touch it." He stood at the door and watched her drive away, hoping a couple of days at her sister's would calm her.

The exterminator arrived at noon on Friday—a tall, skinny guy in blue coveralls that read *Buzz Off Pest Control* across the back. He introduced himself as Marcus.

"The job ticket didn't say exactly what the problem was," Marcus said.

Simon scratched his chin. "Yeah, my wife saw bugs in one of the rooms upstairs. She wouldn't let me open the door to have a look myself—worried the things would get out and infest the rest of the rooms, I guess."

"Fair enough. But most insects can easily find their way under a closed door. Let's go see what you've got. I can check adjacent rooms too, just to make sure they haven't spread."

Simon led Marcus up the steps. Before they reached the top, the phone behind the bar began to ring. "Damn. I should get that."

"No worries," Marcus said. "What room is it?"

"Four, at the end of the hall, there." Simon pointed, then hurried back down the stairs to answer the phone.

He was just hanging up again when a door slammed upstairs, and Marcus, white-faced, jogged down the stairs.

"That bad?" Simon joked.

Marcus swallowed. "Um. Can I use your phone? I need to ring my boss."

"Sure. Is everything okay? What did you find up there?"

"I'm … to be honest, I'm not entirely sure. Your phone?" The man was visibly shaken. What the hell was up there?

Marcus dialled a number, and Simon tried not to eavesdrop—or at least he tried not to *look* like he was eavesdropping. He wiped down tables that were already clean in the dining area in order to be close enough to hear Marcus.

"Yeah, Jim, it's Marcus. Look, I'm at the Rifton Pub and—" he lowered his voice, and Simon missed what came after. Dammit. He moved to a closer table.

"… never seen anything like this … size of cats …" Marcus's words were mostly inaudible, muttered into the receiver. He was silent for a minute, then said, "I don't think it's safe. And what if they get out?" More silence. "Yeah. Yeah. I'll check. Then what do you reckon? Methyl bromide? Yeah, I'm sure I've got some plastic. If we have to do the whole building though … Yeah. Okay. Thanks." He hung up and turned around to face Simon. "Ah … we seem to have an … unusual situation up there in Room Four."

Simon stuffed his cloth into the pocket of his apron. "Unusual?"

"Yeah. It's a pest we haven't encountered before. I'm afraid we need to take aggressive measures to make sure it doesn't spread. It may be a biosecurity risk."

"By aggressive, you mean …" Aggressive almost certainly meant expensive.

"Well, first I need to make sure the infestation hasn't spread beyond the one room. Then we'll need to fumigate the room, which entails sealing it first, then pumping it full of methyl bromide."

Simon didn't know what the hell methyl bromide was, but it sounded bad. "And how long will that take?"

Marcus grimaced. "We'll need everyone out of the building, even with the room sealed, just in case there's a leak. The fumigation takes twenty-four hours, and then we'll vent the room. It'll maybe be two days before anyone can re-enter the building."

Shit. He was going to have to close the pub for two days? Weekend days, at that. "Can you put it off until Monday?"

Marcus shook his head. "There's a new law—the Biosecurity Act. My boss is looking into what our responsibilities are, because whatever you've got up there is almost certainly new to New Zealand. But he doesn't want to mess around here. I'll seal the room this afternoon, and then I'll need to go back to our chemical store and collect the methyl bromide. Hopefully we can get this under way by the end of the day today."

"But it's Friday. I run a pub."

"Look, mate. The things infesting that room? You

want to kill them *now*. Trust me." Marcus looked like he might vomit. "How long have they been there, anyway?"

"My wife noticed them Tuesday morning when she went up to change the sheets. She came down pretty shaken up."

"Did someone stay in the room Monday night?"

"Yeah." Simon thought back to Mrs Hettrick. Could she have brought these things in? She seemed like a nice enough person—a clean person.

"You might want to pull out their contact details and give them a ring while I seal up the room." Marcus headed to his van to collect the equipment he needed.

Simon dialled the number Mrs Hettrick had given him when she checked in. Instead of ringing, he got the message, *The number you have dialled is no longer in service.*

The government officials who arrived on Monday morning took away every one of the insects they could find. Simon never saw the creatures, only noted the half-dozen rubbish bags it took to carry them all.

He shuddered. That was the *last* time he'd ever rent out a hotel room. When the pub was declared pest-free, he went upstairs to survey the scene. The room was a mess—the duvet was torn, the pillow disgorging feathers, and brown stains marred the floor and walls. Some sort of grainy substance had been strewn around the carpet, along with four tealight candles that must have been stepped on, and were now ground into the carpet fibres. The room smelled rank and musty.

Simon hauled every scrap of furniture out to the skip and tipped it in. Then he tore up the carpet and tossed it as well. He scrubbed the walls and the bare wood floor, even wiped down the ceiling. He gave the floor a fresh coat of polyurethane, and painted the walls and ceiling a crisp white. Then he shut and locked the door, tossing the key into the back of his desk drawer and vowing not to open the room again.

# Chapter 12

## *Drunk and Disorderly*

"Katie?" Lane, one of Katie's line cooks, stepped into the kitchen through the back door. "I think you need to come out here." Lane had been out the back on his break.

Katie frowned. She quickly washed her hands and followed Lane out the door.

"What? Again?" A police cruiser, lights flashing, sat in the car park blocking a blue sedan. Two constables stood beside the cruiser, one talking on his radio, the other writing out a citation. A rock settled into Katie's stomach as she strode over to the men. Putting on her most professional voice, she asked, "What's the trouble here, constables?"

The cop who was writing looked up as he tore the citation off his pad. "You the owner?"

"Of the Tipsy Teapot? Yes."

"Let me finish this, and then we'll talk." The cop walked to the driver's side of the blue sedan and handed the ticket through the window. "Next time, get a room." His partner moved the cruiser into a parking space, and the blue sedan drove away. The young man at the wheel was beet red, and the woman in the passenger seat held a hand over her eyes.

What the hell had happened? Katie waited impatiently as the constable chatted briefly with his partner before returning to her. He was an older guy, around her dad's age, she guessed. Tall and broad-shouldered, with a middle-aged paunch. She felt tiny next to him. She pulled herself to her full height and stuck out her hand, refusing to be intimidated. "Hi. I'm Katie Cochrane."

The officer's hand dwarfed hers as he gave it a perfunctory shake. "Constable Basil Shepherd." He glanced at the pub. "You've done a lot of work on the place, haven't you? Business good? Selling a lot of beer?"

Katie couldn't help hearing the slightly accusatory note in Constable Shepherd's voice. "What happened here this evening?"

"A young couple exiting your establishment decided it was a good idea to have sex in the car park. In the middle of the car park. In fact, they never even made it as far as their car."

In other circumstances, Katie would have laughed. Instead, she was dismayed. "And you think they were drunk? I can assure you, sir, my staff are well trained, and we refuse to serve people who are visibly intoxicated. Did you test them?"

"I did."

"And?" Dammit, was he *trying* to make her uncomfortable? *She* wasn't the one who was caught fucking in the car park.

"Their blood alcohol level was slightly elevated."

"But not so high you didn't let them drive away." She had him there. If they'd actually been drunk, he would have prevented them from driving.

"Miss Cochrane, this isn't the first incident at the Tipsy Teapot."

Katie crossed her arms, then uncrossed them—she didn't need to appear antagonistic to a police officer. "I was assured the fight two weeks ago had been deemed unrelated to the limited amount of alcohol those men consumed here, and the woman on the car had been drinking lime and tonic."

"The woman on the car?" The cop raised his eyebrows.

Damn. Why did she have to say anything? The police hadn't been involved in that one. She waved a hand, as if to dismiss her comment. "A woman fell off the roof of her car the other day. Broke her leg."

"Why was she on the roof of her car?"

"Who knows? The point is, she hadn't had a drop of alcohol. I guarantee my staff aren't serving intoxicated people."

"Well, I hope not. If you're right, we won't be seeing you again. Have a good evening, Miss Cochrane."

Katie frowned as the police car pulled out of the car park. When she turned back towards the building, Lane was waiting for her.

"Bit of sexism going on there?" Lane asked. "I didn't hear what he said but his body language, and yours, was clear."

"And probably racism—the little Asian girl obviously doesn't know how to run a bar. Constable Basil Shepherd is an arsehole."

Lane chuckled. "Yeah. But you know his opinion of you doesn't matter. You're awesome at what you do."

Katie snorted.

"No, really. Katie, I've worked in five different kitchens, and yours is by far the best-run place I've ever seen. It's a pleasure to work here."

A little of Katie's tension eased. "Thanks, Lane. It means a lot to me that my staff seem happy at work."

They headed back inside to the familiar chaos of the kitchen, and Katie let go of her anger to focus on her staff and customers.

The following day, Katie received two unwelcome emails. The first was from the police, indicating that they had registered an incident at the Tipsy Teapot in which drunk patrons acted inappropriately upon leaving her establishment and reminding her of her duties under the Sale and Supply of Alcohol Act 2012. It was a warning only, but it pissed Katie off—she *knew* those people hadn't been drunk.

The second unwelcome email came from the district council. The subject line read: *Abatement Notice*.

*On the evening of 7 November, two noise complaints were laid against patrons in the car park of the Tipsy Teapot. The security officer sent to investigate the complaints was unable to locate the offenders. Please be aware that licensed establishments are required to comply with the Sale and Supply of Alcohol Act 2012 and not serve intoxicated patrons. Penalty for non-compliance can result in reduced trading hours, or suspension of your alcohol licence.*

Katie swore. What was up with people in Rifton? Were they all idiots? She didn't remember having these sorts of problems at the places she'd worked in town. Of course, she wouldn't have had to deal with these problems then—she was just a chef.

That evening, she met with Taine and Tui. "I'm going to work the bar and register with you two for a few days," she said. "I want to document exactly what's going on in here, so we can rule out any mistakes on our part. I'm going to keep track of how many drinks people have, what folks are drinking, how full you're filling their glasses—everything."

Taine frowned. "Do you not trust me to know my job?"

"I absolutely trust you, Taine. But if people keep doing stupid shit in our car park, I could lose my liquor licence. I need to have proof we're not in any way responsible for the idiocy of our customers."

"Fair enough."

Tui squeezed Katie's shoulder. "We got this, girl. They can't take away your licence. I'll keep a tally of the number of people in each party and how many drinks they've purchased. The register records the drinks on each bill, but not how many people those drinks are spread over."

"Thanks. That will be helpful."

It was a typical Wednesday—lots of families with children, a few groups of retired folks, and a smattering of couples of all ages out for a drink or a meal. Taine served beers, wine, and one gin and tonic. Katie snapped photos of him setting the filled glasses on the bar—not one of them overfilled. She strolled around the dining area, pretending to tidy things while surreptitiously watching customers. Everyone she saw was sober. Most were eating food along with their beer or wine. The atmosphere was pleasant, calm, and civilised.

When she checked in with Tui, her friend's numbers matched what Katie had observed. "No one has had more than one drink tonight. In fact, I think" —Tui tapped a few numbers into a calculator she carried in her apron— "yep. Our average number of drinks per adult customer this evening is currently at zero point six eight. Hardly a swill fest."

"Good," Katie replied. "Keep recording it. It's probably the last two hours of the day that are the most critical."

Tui nodded. "More drinking, less eating."

By nine-thirty, half an hour before closing, their average number of drinks per person for the night had risen to just below one. As far as Katie could tell, the maximum number of drinks anyone had was two. She was just about to cease her vigilance and head upstairs to get a little paperwork done before closing when a man in uniform walked through the door.

Tui swore under her breath, and Katie's stomach sank.

"Maybe he's just here for a beer after his shift," Taine said hopefully.

But Katie's hopes were dashed as the man approached the bar like he was on a mission, not like a guy who wanted a drink. The insignia on his shirt read, *Foxtrot Security*.

"May I speak to the manager please?" he asked Tui, at the register.

"That's me. How can I help you?" Katie said, stepping out from behind the bar.

"We've had an incident in the car park," the man began. He sounded apologetic, and Katie tried not to take her frustration out on him—it was clear he was just doing his job.

She reined in her emotions. "What happened?"

"We had a noise complaint, and I was sent to check it out. By the time I got here, the situation had ... escalated."

*Shit.* "Escalated?"

The man really did seem sorry to be the bearer of bad news. "Um, so the noise was some guy proselytising in the car park. He apparently got a whole group of people gathered around him, shouting and chanting. That's when the noise complaint was called in. But when a neighbour came out to tell them to pipe down, the crowd started arguing."

Another fight. This one involving more than just two guys. "The police?"

"Are outside and would like to talk to you."

Katie nodded, and the man turned to leave. She stopped him. "Wait. Which officers are out there?"

"Constables Belmont and Daniels. Why?"

Thank God for small favours. "No reason. I was just curious." And in no mood to face Basil Shepherd again. She followed him out the door.

Constables Belmont and Daniels had been polite on Wednesday night, but they warned Katie that it didn't take too many incidents to prompt the district council to suspend liquor licences. So on Thursday, when the fellow from Foxtrot Security again darkened the door of the Tipsy Teapot, Katie wanted to tear her hair out.

"What now?" she said in exasperation.

The man grimaced. "A group of four women singing Christmas carols at top volume in the car park."

"And someone rang the council about it?" Four women singing couldn't make that much noise, could they?

"They had a battery-operated karaoke machine in the car. It was loud."

Katie groaned. "Please tell me the police weren't involved."

"No police tonight—the women left, with a little encouragement."

"You didn't happen to check their blood alcohol levels, did you?" Although Katie knew those girls weren't drunk. She'd served them a total of six drinks.

The man shook his head. "I don't have the authority to do that."

Of course he didn't. Katie almost wished the police had been called—they would have gotten proof the women weren't intoxicated. She pinched the bridge of her nose, a headache coming on.

The man's voice gentled. "You can expect something from the council tomorrow."

Katie nodded. "Yeah. Thanks."

By Friday night, Katie was almost ready to hire her own security guard to hang out in the car park and head off any problems.

"Could someone be doing this on purpose?" Tui asked as she tied on her apron.

"You mean someone who doesn't want me to have a liquor licence?" Katie replied.

"Yeah. Someone who wants to shut down the pub."

"Why would anyone do that? And anyway, it's different people causing different kinds of trouble every night. They can't all be doing it on purpose, can they?"

Tui shrugged. "Maybe they're being paid to do it?"

Katie frowned. She hadn't considered the possibility of malicious neighbours trying to shut her down. It wasn't like Rifton was new to having a pub in town—the Rifton Pub was opened in 1890. If it wasn't welcome, it wouldn't have lasted a hundred and thirty-three years.

Was it *her* they didn't want? At the thought, Katie began angrily scrubbing the bar down. She didn't look up until a large form settled in a stool at the bar opposite where she stood.

"Clean enough yet?"

Katie raised her eyes. Finn Laird quirked an eyebrow at her.

"I don't know what that counter did to you, but you've probably punished it enough." His lips twitched.

Katie knew he was trying to joke with her. Part of her wanted to laugh. But instead, she scowled.

*He's a customer, Katie. Smile!*

She stretched her face into the appropriate shape. "What can I get you, Finn? The usual?"

"Yes please." She felt his eyes on her as she pulled his beer.

"You okay?"

Katie checked her smile—yep, still there. "Fine, thanks, and you?"

His eyes narrowed. "It's just that normally, you would have tried to convince me to order chips or spring rolls or dinner by now."

Katie's smile relaxed into something more natural, and she handed him his beer. "Maybe I've given up. It's clear you're on some sort of a diet. Or your wife or girlfriend has dinner on the table by the time you get home and you don't want to spoil it."

Finn snorted, nearly spitting out the beer in his mouth. "No diet, no wife." He sighed. "No girlfriend."

Katie raised her eyebrows at the sigh—the word girlfriend had obviously hit a sore spot. "Husband?" she suggested. Out of the corner of her eye, she noted Tui, hanging on every word of their conversation.

Finn laughed. "No husband, either. Or boyfriend."

It was Katie's first good news of the week, and it did a great deal to lift her spirits. "So ... what's your excuse? Don't tell me you don't like chips." Katie's stress eased a little with the flirty banter. Her life had been so serious lately.

He had a nice smile. "Caught. You're right. I have no excuse. Could I please have an order of chips?"

"Of course you may." Katie gave him a genuine smile as she handed him the EFTPOS machine so he could swipe his card.

She turned to find Tui smirking in her direction. Katie squeezed past her friend a minute later to refill her stash of serviettes at the bar. "Nice going," Tui whispered in her ear. "A little slower than your usual, though. Normally by this point you've got a date."

Katie rolled her eyes. "Who's got time for dating?" she

whispered back. "I was just being ... a little flirty."

"So, he's got no girlfriend. What else have you found out about him? Have you stalked him online yet?" Tui asked.

Katie nodded. "He likes mountain biking, and his uncle owns Beefy Bernard's in Darfield."

"Why is he drinking here, then?" Tui shifted her attention to an approaching customer.

Katie frowned. She hadn't thought about it before, but it *was* strange Finn was frequenting The Tipsy Teapot when she was sure old Uncle Bernard would give him mates' rates on beer at his place.

Was he coming here to see her? The thought gave Katie a thrill.

Tui finished with her customer and turned back to Katie. "What if he's spying on you for his uncle? What if" —her eyes widened— "*he's* the one sabotaging your business?"

That popped Katie's bubble. Could the owner of Beefy Bernard's want to shut her down? The Tipsy Teapot *was* the closest competition, but ... "You think Finn and his uncle are responsible for the drunks in my car park? That's pretty far-fetched."

"Not really. I bet his business has dropped off since you opened."

Katie shook her head. She'd seen rivalries between restaurants before, but it was always about personalities— owners who had personal rivalries with each other or bad blood between them. "Having other restaurants near yours is usually a good thing. They bring in more customers for everyone."

Tui looked unconvinced. "Maybe this Bernard dude doesn't know that."

Not possible. Katie dismissed the idea. It was far more comforting to think Finn was here to see her than to sabotage her business for his uncle.

There wasn't time for pondering Finn's motivations on a Friday evening. Taine was late for his shift, and there was a birthday party scheduled for seven o'clock, so Katie was busy fixing drinks. She did have a chance to smile at Finn a couple of times when she looked up from her work and found him watching her.

She counted it a win when he smiled back. Surely that meant he was here for her, and not for sabotage, right?

By the time he stood, gave her a nod and left, Katie was feeling lighter than she had all week.

Thirty minutes later, her feel-good bubble burst when Constable Basil Shepherd walked in the door and made a beeline for Katie.

# Chapter 13

## *Stakeout*

"And *then* Constable Shepherd had the fucking gall to accuse me of selling drugs!" Katie stomped down the pavement beside Alex on their Saturday morning walk, recounting the events of the week.

"He *what*?" How could someone accuse Katie of dealing drugs? Alex couldn't imagine a less likely person to engage in illegal behaviour of any kind.

"He didn't straight up say it, but he may as well have. When the breath alcohol test once again showed that the troublemakers weren't drunk, he said, 'Well, they were intoxicated by *something*. You serving anything else in that pub?' I told him I'd be happy to bring him a menu if he wanted to know."

Alex laughed at Katie's cheeky response. Then she frowned. "What I don't understand is why you're having so many problems with unruly behaviour in the car park. I don't remember there being big problems before." Not that she paid much attention as a teenager, but she thought she would have known if the pub had a reputation as a rowdy place.

"I don't get it either." Katie sounded dejected. "My friend Tui thinks it's deliberate—someone trying to sabotage my business."

"Who would do that?"

Katie shrugged. "Tui thinks it's the owner of Beefy Bernard's in Darfield. I don't think so." She was silent for a few steps. "I don't know anyone specifically who would want to ruin my business. Maybe it's racism—it's not like there are a lot of Asians in Rifton."

Alex opened her mouth to say it couldn't be racism. Then she shut it again, remembering the shit the one Indian boy in her high school class had been subjected to. As much as she didn't want to believe it, it wasn't a completely unrealistic conjecture.

"I'm thinking I might need to hire a security guard," Katie continued, "but I'm not sure how I'm going to afford it. Business is good, but I'm still trying to make back all my start-up costs."

Poor Katie. She shouldn't have to be dealing with this rubbish. "What if Shel and I staked out the car park this evening? Just to see what's happening. It could be that the noise complaints are bogus."

"Maybe, but there have been fights, injuries—"

"Yeah, but most of the incidents have been things someone could make up. If a neighbour has a bee in their bonnet and is calling in every little squeak from the car park as a noise complaint, it would explain a lot of your troubles."

"I can't ask you to sit around in the car park. I'll hire a security guard."

"Honest, it's not a problem. Shel and I were planning on dinner at the Tipsy Teapot this evening anyway. We'll just hang out in the car park for a while afterwards. Even having people there might help—if there are witnesses, maybe the people causing trouble will think twice about doing it."

"I suppose it can't hurt. If you don't mind. Really. I feel bad that you're even offering."

"Nonsense. It'll be fun. We'll take our coffee and dessert out there and make it a picnic."

Katie laughed. "Coffee and dessert will be on the house, okay?"

"Deal."

They parted ways shortly after, Katie turning towards the Tipsy Teapot, and Alex heading home to chat with Shel about the evening's plan.

It was a beautiful evening—the sun slanted down between pink-tinged clouds while the day's warmth slowly ebbed. Alex and Shel had driven to the Tipsy Teapot, though it was only two blocks from home—they'd decided it would be less awkward to hang out in the car park if they had a vehicle to sit in.

Armed with large takeaway coffees and oversized slices of carrot cake, they began their stakeout, sitting in the car with a view of the car park. They rolled down the windows, and a light breeze carried the smell of freshly mown grass. It was more pleasant than Alex expected.

Alex took a bite of her cake. "Oh my god, this is amazing! The icing is so flavourful."

"Did Katie make it?" Shel asked before biting into his own piece.

Alex shook her head. "I think it's Katie's recipe, but her pastry chef, Jill, has been doing all the baking lately. Katie's only making the icing—she's been walking with me in the mornings instead of helping with the baking."

Shel grunted, his mouth full of cake. After swallowing, he said, "Why isn't Jill doing the icing too?"

Alex laughed. "Some challenge Sharon has put her up to—to create the perfect carrot cake. Apparently Sharon has yet to approve the icing."

As they ate, Shel and Alex watched. The dinnertime rush was going strong, and the car park was busy with people arriving and leaving. Families, groups of friends, couples—they came and went. Most moved quickly through the car park and didn't linger.

"Well, it looks pretty good so far," Shel said. "Maybe it'll be a quiet night."

Alex took a sip of her coffee. "It's only seven-thirty. Katie said it's usually nine or later when the trouble starts."

They finished their cake and coffee, chatting about this and that, eyes roving the car park as the sun set, washing the whole sky in magenta and orange.

A group of four men sauntered out of the pub and headed to their car at the far end of the car park. They were laughing and joking. As they passed Alex and Shel, they were discussing whether to play pool at one of the men's houses or drive into Christchurch to see a movie.

They stood by their car for a minute, still talking, and their volume rose. From one moment to the next, their friendly conversation turned to a heated fight. They shouted and swore at one another, and Alex was just about to suggest she and Shel go over and try to diffuse the situation when they got into their car and drove off.

"Well, that was weird," Alex said.

"Yeah, especially the plants," added Shel.

"The plants?"

"You didn't notice them?" Shel met Alex's gaze.

"I assume you mean the plants the garden group suspects are demons. No. I didn't notice them. I was focused on the men."

"When those guys got close to them, the plants started moving. At first I thought it was the wind."

"But there's no wind." Alex felt a prickling on the back of her neck.

"Exactly. The guys stood there at their car, and the plants waved their branches at them."

"They were trying to attack the men?" The prickling erupted as goosebumps all over Alex's arms.

Shel shook his head. "I'm not sure they were attacking. But they were definitely reacting to the presence of the men."

A young couple walked past on the way to their car. Alex watched carefully, eyes flicking between the couple and the strange plants as the pair came nearer to the plants.

Their car was parked in front of a mystery plant, and as they reached the passenger side door, the plant began to sway, leaves quivering as if a stiff breeze blew. The man opened the door for the woman and bent down to kiss her as he did so. The plant continued to sway.

The kiss, which started as a quick peck, devolved rapidly into heavy groping, and soon the man was unbuttoning the woman's shirt.

Alex jumped out of the car and slammed her door shut. At the sound, the couple's heads shot up. The shocked looks on their faces were almost comical. The woman ducked into the car, hastily buttoning her shirt. The man slunk around the car to the driver's side, hands in his pockets.

Alex climbed back into the car as the couple drove off. She met Shel's wide-eyed gaze.

"What the hell?" Shel's Adam's apple bobbed as he swallowed.

Alex thought for a moment. The men's conversation didn't turn into an argument until they were at their car, near the strange plants. The couple hadn't even been holding hands until they reached their car, near the plants. "Shel, do you think the plants are making people act drunk in the car park?"

A family of five exited the pub. Alex held her breath as she watched. The kids skipped. Mum and Dad held the children's hands, told them to be careful in the car park. Their car was parked far from the plants, and when they reached it, the kids piled in, followed by Mum and Dad, and they drove off.

Alex released her breath. "Well? What do you think?"

"You may be right," Shel agreed.

The next five groups to exit the pub had parked varying distances from the plants. They left without incident, and the plants didn't move.

Maybe she and Shel had imagined the plants moving, the people's behaviour changing.

Shortly after, several groups came out of the pub at the same time, and Alex couldn't keep track of them all. Two groups—a gaggle of six middle-aged women and a family of three—headed towards the far side of the car park, towards the strange plants.

The plants shivered and swayed as the people approached. The family quickly hopped into their car and drove away. The group of women, who had clearly arrived in multiple cars, stopped to continue their conversation when they reached their vehicles.

Alex couldn't hear their conversation, but they all laughed at something, and then one of them dropped into the driver's seat of her car and started revving the engine. Soon they were all in their cars, acting like boy racers. The noise was deafening as engines screamed, and then they peeled out of the car park with squealing tyres, leaving black streaks of rubber behind.

"It has to be the plants," Shel said.

"Let's test it." Alex opened her door.

Shel grabbed her arm. "Wait. How?"

"I'm going to walk over there and stand near the plants. You stay here and watch what I do."

"I don't like it." Shel didn't release her.

"I'll be fine. All you have to do is watch." Alex detached her arm from Shel's grip and got out of the car. Before shutting her door, she paused and turned back to him. "If I ... ah ... do anything embarrassing, can you come rescue me?"

"Of course."

Alex strode across the car park, eyes on the plants. As she expected, they began to sway as she drew near. What were they doing? They didn't seem to be reaching towards her, though she swore those weird leaves at the ends of the branches were snapping like crab claws. As the branches swayed, the bell-shaped flowers swung back and forth.

Two metres from the plants, Alex was hit by the smell—cloying and sweet, like breathing treacle. Was the perfume making people act drunk? She suppressed the urge to hold her breath—the whole idea was to determine if the plants were affecting people. She forced her lungs to expand, drawing the scent in.

She stopped just out of reach of the plants' swaying branches, watching closely to see if they were doing anything other than swaying and perfuming the air. She was so focused on the plants that she barely registered the car pulling in to a space next to where she stood. The people got out, and one of them commented, "I'm so hungry I could eat a horse."

Horse? Alex had never had horse meat. Was it good? She should get some and try it. Even after a meal and a big dessert, she thought she could eat again, and horse sounded great. Alex jogged back to Shel's car and jumped in.

"Anything?" he asked.

"Not that I noticed. I feel fine. Not drunk at all. Come on.

Let's go get some horse meat."

"Horse meat?" Shel frowned at her.

"Yeah! Is the grocery store still open? Maybe the dairy will have it? Or do you have to go to the butcher to get that?"

"Why do you want horse meat?"

Alex frowned. "Why *wouldn't* you want horse meat? I hear it's really good. Come on, let's get to the grocery store before they close."

Shel nodded and started the car. "Okaaay." He pulled out of the car park and turned into the neighbourhood.

"Hey, the grocery store's that way," Alex said. "Where are you going?"

"I'm a little chilly. I was gonna pick up my jacket beforehand."

A block away from the pub, Alex shook her head, which she realised felt strange. "Did I just—"

"Ask me to drive you to the store to buy some horse meat?" Shel asked. "Yep."

# Chapter 14

## *Suspicious Shrubbery*

On Monday, when the Tipsy Teapot was closed, Alex invited Katie around for dinner. Katie was eager, and a bit nervous, to talk to her—Alex had refused to tell her much about her and Shel's evening stakeout on Saturday, saying it was a conversation that might take some time.

What could they have seen? Somebody paying patrons to act drunk as they left? A neighbour watching the pub through binoculars? Katie's stomach churned at the thought someone was doing this on purpose.

She knocked on Alex's door, unsurprised when Shel opened it and ushered her in. The black cat, Thor, was there again, wrapping himself around her ankles as she stepped into the house.

"Hi Katie!" Alex waved an oven-mitt-clad hand in Katie's direction. She opened the oven and a billow of deliciously scented steam wafted out.

"Oh my god, that smells delicious," Katie said, setting a bottle of wine and a plate of cookies on the kitchen bench.

Alex shrugged. "I just made quesadillas."

Katie smiled. "Tin of beans, jar of salsa and some cheese folded into a wrap? The best of flatting food!"

Alex laughed and slid the quesadillas off the tray onto a

platter. "Exactly! One of my flatmates taught me how to make these. I think I've made them weekly since."

"And here I thought this was a culinary school secret."

"Well, I'd never had one until Alex made them," Shel said.

"Come on. Let's eat on the deck." Alex picked up the tray. "Can you grab some glasses, Shel? Bring the wine and cookies, Katie."

They settled in the deckchairs. Katie was bursting with questions, but restrained herself as they tucked into their quesadillas.

Alex popped the last of her quesadilla into her mouth, wiped her hands, and picked up her wine glass. "So, I expect you want to know what happened Saturday night."

"Yes please." Katie could hear the desperation in her own voice. "Although I'm not looking forward to hearing who is trying to harm my business."

"We're pretty certain no one is deliberately trying to shut you down," Shel said as he picked up his second quesadilla.

Alex drew in a breath. "But I'm not sure you're going to like what we found out."

"If you even *believe* it," Shel added.

Now Katie was confused. What on earth had they discovered?

They told her the story of their stakeout, how the unusual plants near the car park were apparently intoxicating people who spent too much time near them.

Katie relaxed. "Well, that's strange, but it's easily solved. I'll just rip the plants out."

Alex and Shel shared a look—clearly there was more.

"I don't think you should try that," Alex said.

"I don't think you *can* do it, even if you tried," Shel added.

"The plants aren't that big. I'm sure I can buy a pruning saw and—"

Alex shook her head. "They're not actually plants. If you try to cut them down, they'll probably bite you."

Bite?

"The garden group has already tried to take cuttings from them and failed," Shel said.

"What do you mean, they're not plants?" Katie couldn't make head nor tail of what Alex and Shel were saying.

"We—the garden group and us—think they're demons." Alex took a sip of her wine.

Well, that wasn't the answer Katie was expecting. She blinked at Alex. Surely the woman was joking. But her face remained solemn.

"Demons, as in monsters from Hell?" Katie asked, just to make sure there wasn't some definition of demon she didn't know about.

Alex nodded. "I'm pretty sure they're not from Hell, but they *are* from a different dimension or world."

"At least we assume so. The others have been." Shel took a sip of wine.

"The others?" This was getting weird.

Alex gave a little sigh. "Pour yourself another glass of wine. You might need it."

Alex and Shel then proceeded to tell Katie the most unbelievable story about how Alex had accidentally summoned a demon from a book her grandmother owned, which she pulled out and showed to Katie. During their efforts to return the demon to its own world, they discovered that the cat, Thor, was also a demon.

"And how does the garden group come into all this?" Katie asked.

"Gran was one of the members of the group," Alex said. "They're the ones who summoned Thor. They also summoned another cat demon, who lives with Margaret."

"They purposely summoned demons?" Katie eyed Thor who looked like nothing more than an ordinary house cat sprawled across Shel's legs.

"Yeah, don't get me started on that. Gran summoned Thor to spy on me after I ran away from home."

"And why do you think the plants in my car park are demons?" A cat and a plant weren't exactly similar. And what the hell? Katie struggled to wrap her head around the idea.

"Both Shel and Pauline were bitten by them," Alex said.

"*Bitten?*"

Alex nodded. "That, and the whole intoxication thing. And the speed of their growth. And the fact they seem to move around."

Katie laughed. What else could she do? This was completely ridiculous. She hadn't pegged Alex and Shel as the type to believe in stupid stuff like demons, but they were serious about this. "I'm sure there's some other explanation. They're just plants."

Alex shrugged. "We're telling you what we saw and experienced. Regardless of what they are, they're the source of your problems."

"Well, thanks for that. Now that I know the problem, I can deal with it." Katie changed the subject. She didn't want to listen to more crackpot nonsense about demons. It was a shame that Alex and Shel turned out to be so ... weird. She'd started to really like them. Now she wasn't so sure.

The obvious solution to Katie's problem was to remove the plants, but they'd grown to the size of large shrubs, and she'd need to buy some tools to do the job. She didn't have time to run to the city until Thursday, so in the meantime, she roped off that side of the car park to keep patrons away from the plants.

How far away did people need to be? Katie approached a plant. Its leaves fluttered in the breeze, and the large red flowers swung like bells. They were striking plants—put those flowers in a big vase, and they'd make amazing Christmas decorations.

About two metres from the plant, she smelled its cloying, sweet perfume. That must be what intoxicated people. She stepped away until she could no longer smell it, then strung a rope between chairs to prevent people from parking in the spaces nearby. That would have to do until she removed the plants.

That evening, business was steady but manageable—a typical Tuesday, with lots of retired couples, a few families. Content that her staff had everything under control, Katie was about to retreat to the office to catch up on paperwork when Finn Laird walked through the doorway.

On a Tuesday? Tui's suspicions about him flared in Katie's mind. Was he here to sabotage her? No. Alex and Shel had determined it was the intoxicating plants making people act weird. Of course, they also said the plants were demons. It wouldn't hurt to keep an eye on Finn. She nudged Tui off for her break as Finn sat down at the bar.

"This isn't your usual night," she said to him.

He smiled. "Nope, but I'll have the usual beer."

"Sure you don't want some chips or dinner with that beer?"

"No thank you."

It was time to push. See if she could get anything from him. Katie wasn't sure what she wanted—a confession he was spying for his uncle, or an invitation to a date. "Do you ever eat?"

He laughed. "I got chips the other day."

Katie snorted. "Chips. Once. What was wrong with the chips? What's wrong with the food at my restaurant that you won't eat it?" She was confident there was nothing wrong with her menu, but she needed to find out more about Finn. She didn't want to ask outright why he was here and not at his uncle's restaurant—that would be admitting she'd stalked him online. Not good if he was spying on her, embarrassing if he was interested in her, and mortifying if he wasn't.

"I'm sure the food here is fine. But it seems silly to order food when I'm not hungry."

"Well, the obvious solution is to skip lunch then, isn't it?" Katie said before sidling away to ring up a customer.

The elderly couple from table fourteen smiled when Katie asked if they'd enjoyed their meal.

"Oh yes, it was delicious, thank you."

Katie logged into the cash register and tried to key in their order. The screen flashed an error message: *E026 Enter Condiment/preparation PLU*. What the hell was that? She frowned and hit the clear key. The error message vanished, and she tried to put the sale through again. The same error message came up.

"Sorry, the machine seems to be acting up on me here. Give me a moment," Katie said.

Three more tries, with the same error message began to fluster Katie.

"It's alright love. We're not in a hurry," the elderly woman said kindly. Katie gave her a harried smile.

"Can I help?" Finn stood and walked over to her.

"What? No thanks. I can manage." She really couldn't let a customer come around the bar. And certainly not Finn— what if he *was* trying to sabotage her? Giving him access to the register was a bad idea.

"What sort of error is it giving you?" Finn asked, leaning forward.

Katie didn't respond, trying to put the sale through once more.

*E026 Enter Condiment/preparation PLU.*

*Shit.* Katie suppressed a growl of frustration.

"You sure I can't help?" Finn asked. His slightly amused look only increased Katie's irritation.

"Sorry, but I can't let a customer mess around with our cash register." Katie punched at the keys, trying to work out what she'd done wrong.

Finn smiled and pulled a business card out of his wallet. He handed the card to Katie. "Finn Laird, POS sales and service representative—it's my job to sell and fix cash registers. May I help you?"

Katie shut her eyes for a moment, considering. She knew *nothing* about cash registers. It had taken her all day and several desperate queries on Reddit to set up the second-hand register she'd bought. Flustered, and with a customer waiting, she knew she wasn't going to solve this problem on her own. She opened her eyes and waved Finn around the bar. "Well, then, go for it."

Finn stepped up to the machine, cancelled the sale, keyed the machine to programming mode and started pressing buttons like he'd done this operation a hundred times. Maybe he had. Katie watched closely, making sure he wasn't doing anything destructive—not that she'd necessarily know if he was—and trying to memorise his keystrokes so she could troubleshoot the problem herself if it happened again.

Within moments, Finn stepped back. "Give it a go now. Should work."

Katie stepped up and put the transaction through with no

problem, keenly aware of Finn leaning over her shoulder making sure it worked.

The elderly couple paid and left. Katie huffed out a breath and turned to Finn, who took a step back. "Thank you. It might easily have taken me half an hour to figure out how to fix that."

"No worries. It's not an uncommon error on these older machines."

Katie smiled, her tension easing. He hadn't sabotaged her. Of course, he was a freaking cash register salesperson—no doubt there was an ulterior motive to his help. "And now I imagine you'll give me some marketing spiel?" She'd bought a second-hand register in order to save money, and she knew there were newer models with lots of great features.

"Nah. I could, of course, if you're interested in upgrading, but there's nothing inherently wrong with these older systems. They just sometimes take a little more troubleshooting." He lingered next to Katie, his eyes on the register.

"Well, thank you again. Your beer's on the house this evening." Then Katie thought about the fact he did this for a living, and added. "Though I'm happy to pay—I don't mean to steal your services."

He smiled at her. "Don't be ridiculous. I was right here, and it was a simple thing for me to do. I'm happy to pay for my beer, too."

"No. I insist. You deserve a free beer for saving me from fighting with that machine." He really was good-looking this close, especially when he smiled down at her. Damn. Out of the corner of her eye, Katie saw Tui round the corner from the kitchen, take in the scene, freeze, and then tiptoe back. That girl!

"Well, in that case, I suppose my work here is done." Finn

flashed her a smile. "See you Friday."

Katie watched Finn leave, a little bit dazed by his presence.

Tui shot out of the kitchen. "Do I dare ask what that was?"

Katie snorted. "It was Finn Laird, cash register sales and serviceman, fixing our register when it broke on me just now."

"Looked like more than that. Do you mean to tell me you *still* don't have a date with him?"

"You don't still suspect him of sabotage?" Katie asked.

Tui shrugged. "Once you two start dating, he'll back off on the sabotage."

Katie snorted. "I don't think he's spying for his uncle. But there's not much point in trying to get a date when I work every waking hour of every day." Although, if Finn asked, Katie might make the time. To change the subject, she asked, "All quiet in the car park?" Tui would have been in the staff break area overlooking it.

"All good."

Thank God.

After Tuesday's uneventful evening, Katie was feeling relaxed on Wednesday. So when Officer Smith walked through the door, she waved a cheery hello before registering that he wouldn't be here in uniform if he was here as a customer.

Shit. Her stomach sank. "Please don't tell me there's been another fight in my car park."

"No. Not a fight." The way Officer Smith said the words implied he'd welcome a fight over what had actually happened. "Seems that a group of young people leaving the Tipsy Teapot decided it would be a good idea to tip someone's car onto its side."

"They *what*?" Dammit! She thought she'd solved her problem, at least for the moment.

Hours later, with the car righted and its owner having miraculously driven it out of the car park with little damage besides a few dents and a broken wing mirror, Katie wanted nothing more than to collapse, maybe with a glass of wine in hand.

She locked up and, before heading home, decided to move the barrier rope in the car park. Maybe people needed to be kept back a little further from the plants. She strode to the barrier and began to drag a chair backwards. But something caught her eye. Something red.

She turned her head towards the incongruous colour and dropped the chair. "No. No. That's impossible." On the side of the car park, where yesterday there stood only a motley assortment of poorly tended hedging plants, were two of the mysterious plants. Lush, two metres tall, and covered in big red flowers, they *hadn't been there yesterday*. Two more of the plants, stationary at present, had edged around the corner from the end of the car park Katie had roped off.

They had moved.

"No." Katie said it aloud and with force, trying to convince herself. "Plants can't move." Was someone playing a sick joke on her? She glanced around, expecting to see someone with a shovel and an evil grin on their face standing nearby. But she was alone. At least, it *looked* like she was. For the first time ever, she was nervous about walking home after dark.

She abandoned the idea of moving the barrier, double-checked that she'd locked every door of the pub, and jogged the entire way home, nerves jangling all the way.

Tomorrow morning, she would buy a saw. She'd cut those plants down and chop them into little pieces. Then she'd find out who was tormenting her and make sure they stopped.

# Interlude 5

## *2009*

Margaret dipped a serviette in her water glass and wiped it across the sticky ring on the table in front of her. "You know, we could meet elsewhere now." She would much rather meet in someone's lounge than in the Rifton Pub.

The other women in the garden group made noncommittal noises, and Margaret added, "Liz won't care, now that she's dead."

"But it's tradition to meet here," Sharon argued.

"Only because Liz and Simon used to own the pub and gave us free wine."

"True. And the carrot cake hasn't been the same since Liz passed." Sharon looked forlornly at the listing slice of cake on her plate.

"The place *is* a bit … sticky," Alice admitted, swiping at the table in front of her.

"And you couldn't pay me to step into the ladies' room," Jane added.

"Okay, so I propose we meet at my place next month," Ellen said.

"Fine. Now that that's out of the way, let's eat. I *do* like the apple pie, and if this is our last time meeting here, I don't want to miss out." Pauline rubbed her hands together and picked up her fork.

Ellen inhaled appreciatively over her plate. "I'll miss the curly fries, too."

A large grey cat brushed against Margaret's ankles and she laughed, bent down and picked the animal up, setting it on her lap and stroking its fur. "I'll miss Thunder, too." The pub cat always joined them for their meetings.

"How old do you think Thunder is now?" Alice mused.

Thunder meowed, as if answering.

"Well, Liz always said she'd inherited him with the pub," Ellen began.

"And she bought the pub in 1980," Jane said, waving her fork. "I remember because it was the year Pink Floyd released 'Another Brick in the Wall'."

Alice frowned at Jane. "Why do you associate Pink Floyd with Liz and Simon buying the pub?"

Jane laughed. "I'm a high school teacher. I swear that song was my students' anthem that year, and it made them all stroppy. I started coming down to the pub to do my grading over a glass of wine—it was how I made it through the year."

"That would make Thunder at least twenty-nine years old." Margaret stroked Thunder's healthy, glossy fur. "He certainly doesn't look that old."

Alice's eyes narrowed. "Is that even possible for a cat?"

Possibly, but Margaret was beginning to suspect something about Thunder.

"Maybe living in a pub confers youth." Ellen giggled and popped another curly fry into her mouth.

"Maybe something about *this* pub confers youth," Sharon said around a mouthful of cake. "Remember how Liz used to say there was something strange about Room Four? Something *uncanny*, she said."

Pauline scoffed. "No doubt he's in such good health because Liz used to mix ginseng and turmeric into his food. Both are good for your cardiovascular system, you know. Keeps you young and healthy."

Thunder meowed again. Margaret thought it sounded like a complaint. Did cats dislike ginseng and turmeric? Of course, the cat didn't understand the conversation and couldn't tell them. Unless he could …

"I've been drinking ginger and sage tea for my arthritis recently," remarked Sharon as she finished scraping her plate clean.

"Add some willow bark to it—it'll help a lot," suggested Pauline.

"Has anyone tried that bee sting therapy for arthritis?" Jane shuddered. "I can't imagine allowing myself to be stung on purpose."

The conversation continued, but Margaret's mind was fixed on Thunder. Was there something about the pub that preserved his youth? Why did the cat stay here through multiple owners? And why did Margaret always get the impression the cat *understood* their conversations? Just like her 'cat' Leo did. Liz talked about strange happenings in the pub, but there was something strange about the pub cat, too. He was a lot like Leo.

Should she tell the other women about Leo? About the cat-shaped familiar she'd summoned to help her look after her ageing mother? She'd done the summoning in secret a decade ago and hadn't mentioned her new cat wasn't actually from this world. She'd borrowed Alice's book for the summoning, but didn't think Alice had connected Leo with the book. She worried about what her friends would say if they knew she'd been desperate enough to summon a demon.

She leaned in to Thunder and whispered, "What are you, Thunder? And what about this pub attracts you?" Had Thunder been summoned years ago in this very pub? Who summoned him, and where were they now? Did he stay here in order to get back to wherever he came from?

A stab of guilt lanced through her. She hadn't banished Leo back to his home when her mother died. Truth was, she didn't know how, but she hadn't even tried. She'd grown fond of the cat demon. What would happen to him when she died? Would he be stuck here for the rest of his life? Did he want to go back? She'd never even considered the question, never asked him.

Thunder gazed at her with his amber eyes, as if considering her question. "Meow," he said emphatically, though she didn't understand him.

She could talk to Leo. Could Leo talk to Thunder and find out more about him for her? Maybe she could help Thunder in some way. And she supposed she needed to ask Leo if he wanted to go home. It would break her heart if he did, but she'd been selfish not to consider it earlier.

"I'll do what I can for you," she whispered to Thunder, then tuned back into the conversation which had swirled around her unheeded for the past five minutes.

# Chapter 15

## *Suspended*

*Why* hadn't she just taken the time to cut the bushes down yesterday? Katie slumped in her office chair and stared at the email from the district council. They hadn't wasted any time.

*Dear Ms. Cochrane,* it said. *The district council alcohol licensing board has been notified of two new incidents of drunken conduct outside the Tipsy Teapot, on the evenings of November 16 and 17. These incidents, combined with the string of similar incidents outside your establishment has led to the licensing board's decision to suspend your liquor licence, effective immediately. You are welcome to reapply for a licence, but the success of your application will depend upon you satisfying the board that the conditions giving rise to previous incidents have been rectified.*

It was Friday, and she wasn't allowed to serve alcohol.

"Oh my god! How could this have happened?" Katie gripped her hair, still staring at the email. She'd done nothing wrong, she knew it. How could they take her licence away? How would her business survive? The weight of her business loan had never seemed heavier.

Those damned plants! And whoever had planted them.

Anger flared in Katie's chest. She shoved her chair back as she stood. She'd cut those stupid plants down right now. The

134

new saw was in her hand and she was halfway to the door when a thought stopped her.

If she cut down the plants today and the problems stopped, it would look like alcohol *had* been the problem. She'd never get her licence back.

Then again, if she *didn't* cut the plants down and the problems continued, the council could shut her down completely.

"Damned if I do, damned if I don't." Katie swore. What was she supposed to do? Whoever had done this to her was clever—they'd put her in a position where she couldn't win.

She swore again, thankful none of her staff were in the building yet this morning to hear her. Anger and frustration consumed her thoughts, and her grip on the saw tightened. She needed to get this out of her system so she could calm down and think. Cutting down those bloody plants would do nicely to vent her anger. Brandishing the saw, she stormed down the steps and out to the car park.

The warm late spring sun couldn't calm the storm inside Katie as she approached the first of the plants. The branches of the offending bush began waving as she neared it, and apprehension cooled some of Katie's anger. Was that plant moving on its own? What the hell?

*Don't stop. Just chop the thing down.* Katie ignored her unease and knelt just beyond reach of the swaying branches. She couldn't reach the trunk without getting closer. Alex's warning about the plants flashed through her mind. Would they bite her?

*Come on Katie, that's ridiculous. It's a plant.* Before she could reconsider, she ducked underneath the lowest branch and reached out with the saw, rasping it along the trunk with frenzied motions.

Something stung her ear, her neck, the side of her face.

"Shit!" She dragged herself away from the bush. Out of range, she wiped at the painful flesh. Her hand came away bloodied.

Shaking, she stumbled back even further. What the hell just happened? The bush swayed, as if shaken by a stiff breeze.

Maybe her sawing had simply shaken the tree. The branches would have naturally swayed, and could have easily swatted her across the face and scratched her. That's all. She stepped back further and the plant's swaying died down. Okay, what now? She still needed to cut those things down, but she didn't want to get scratched doing it.

The pruning saw was designed to have a long handle attached. She hadn't purchased the extension handle, but it would be easy to shove a broom handle into the extension slot and screw it in place. Then she could saw without getting near the plants.

Ten minutes later, she was back in the car park with her newly extended saw. Safely out of reach of the branches, she slipped the saw underneath the leaves and dragged it across the trunk.

Instantly, branches began to thrash wildly. Katie redoubled her efforts, sawing madly. Whatever the hell these plants were, they were coming out now.

She couldn't see how deeply her saw was cutting, but she kept working at it. The plant continued to thrash, but its movements weren't the random effects of the sawing. They were deliberate strikes at the saw handle.

That was impossible. A plant couldn't know what was happening. It couldn't purposefully attack a saw—Katie must be imagining it.

But when a large branch, tipped with claw-like leaves, reached down and snapped the broom handle in two, there was no denying it. Katie yelped and jumped back, severed broom in her hand. She held it defensively, as though the plant might follow her as she backed away, muttering a litany of swear words, every nerve jangling. When she reached the edge of the car park, she turned and ran.

Thank God for Alex. When Katie rang her, shaking and nearly incoherent, Alex talked her down and scheduled a meeting with the Rifton garden group.

"They're the closest thing Rifton has to witches. Between us, we'll get rid of the plants. Look, I need to head to work. Are you going to be okay? If you need him, I'm sure Shel could pop over."

Katie took a shaky breath. "No. I'll be fine. Thanks Alex."

The rest of the day was every bit as difficult as she expected. A long and frustrating phone call to the council netted her a meeting for Monday to discuss the licence suspension, but no relief for the weekend. She sent one of her morning staff members to Rolleston to buy out the grocery stores' stocks of low-alcohol beer and wine.

Her staff was every bit as outraged as she was about the loss of their liquor licence, and their support helped. Taine had the brilliant idea of holding an impromptu 'mocktails night', so that people who arrived planning to drink alcohol might be distracted by fancy drinks. "Besides," he said, "lots of mocktails use tea as a base—they're perfect for the Tipsy Teapot."

"You know some good mocktails?" she asked him.

"I know a few, and I know how to use the internet. By the time the dinner crowd arrives I'll have a mocktail menu with something for everyone."

"Thank you!" Katie blinked back tears. "I'm so sorry

about this."

Taine laid a hand on her shoulder. "Katie, this isn't your fault. Between the lack of evidence any of the troublemakers have been intoxicated, and the evidence we've collected in the past week about our customers' drinking, there's nothing they can pin on us. Monday you'll go in there, sort it all out, and by Tuesday, we'll be back in business."

Katie wasn't sure it would be that easy, but that was a worry for Monday. Today, she had to focus on keeping customers happy.

"I'm going to stay out front tonight in order to address any complaints." She wouldn't let her staff take the heat for an issue she should have dealt with earlier.

Katie posted a notice inside the front door, alerting customers there would be no alcohol, and advertising a fun mocktail night. After the first group arrived, saw the notice, and walked out, she moved the notice to the footpath outside—it was too depressing watching the people choose to leave. Better if they did it without her knowing.

By the time Finn Laird arrived for his Friday night beer, Katie's stomach was churning. She'd already had two conversations with disgruntled customers who'd come in to find out why she wasn't serving alcohol and give her a piece of their mind. Like she had any choice! Sure, there was booze behind the bar, but if she was caught serving it, there was no way she'd ever get her licence back.

Finn's frown as he sat down didn't make her feel any better. "I'll deal with him," Katie muttered to Taine.

She knew her smile was fake as she approached Finn at the bar. "What'll it be this evening? We've got a range of mocktails tonight you're not going to want to miss."

"Why no beer?" Finn's tone wasn't accusatory like some of the other customers had been, just curious. Was it personal curiosity, or was he going to turn around and pass the information to his uncle so the man could gloat?

"Temporary problem with our liquor licence." The line she'd told all her staff to use.

Finn's eyes widened, and his look of dismay disarmed Katie. "Was it that woman who fell off her car? Why didn't you ring me?" His tone spoke genuine concern. She needed to stop suspecting him of sabotage.

Katie's facade cracked a little and she shook her head. "No, there have been some other incidents of noise and misconduct in our car park. By people who *weren't* drunk. The council's reaction was to pull our licence." Then she added quickly, "I'm meeting with them Monday, and expect to have it reinstated quickly, because we haven't breached our licence." She hoped she projected more confidence than she felt. Just saying the words struck her as a great way to jinx herself.

She cranked her smile back into place. "So, can I interest you in a mocktail?" She gestured to the mocktail menu Taine had written on a chalkboard above the bar. This was Finn's chance to leave and have a proper beer at his uncle's bar. Katie held her breath, waiting for it.

Finn's gaze lingered for a moment on her face before flicking up to the menu. He studied it and then ordered the Black Goose—a drink Taine had made up from random ingredients they had on hand—blackcurrant juice, fresh gooseberries Jill had bought for pies, fresh lemon juice and soda water. "And can I have an order of chips too?"

A genuine smile spread across Katie's face as she let out her breath. "Without me twisting your arm?"

Finn's mouth quirked up at the corners and he shrugged. "I'm hungry tonight."

On another night, Katie might have used Finn's

admission of hunger to encourage him to buy a meal, something she hadn't yet managed to convince him to do. But tonight, the fact he hadn't bolted to his uncle's place was more than enough for her.

Saturday morning, the entire garden group, plus Alex and Shel, gathered around three tables pushed together before opening time.

"Thank you so much for your help," said Katie as she brought over a tray of coffees and sat down at the remaining chair. "Did Alex tell you what happened yesterday when I tried to cut down one of the plants?"

The women nodded, and Margaret spoke up. "We've been doing some research. I sent Leo down here to have a look, and he says they're definitely demonic."

"Who's Leo?" Katie asked.

"My familiar. He's a demon, looks like a house cat." Margaret's tone was nonchalant, as though discussing your household demon was no big deal. "Anyway, he says they're present, but rare in his world, and he knows little about them."

A cat had confirmed that the plants growing in Katie's car park were demons from another world. Katie took a deep breath to keep from blurting out something sarcastic. Whether she believed these plants came from another world or not, they were decidedly weird. Maybe the cat was right.

"The problem is, we haven't been able to find any information on the summoning or banishment of this particular demon," Pauline said.

"Or any information at all, really," Jane added. "We're not

entirely sure what sort of danger this demon poses, aside from what we've already experienced."

"Isn't that enough? It's made me lose my liquor licence, and it *snapped a broom handle in two!*" Katie wasn't certain the women were taking this matter seriously enough.

Sharon raised a placating hand. "Yeah. It's more than enough. We're actually pretty worried about these things."

"Which is why," Ellen said, "we want to try herbicide while we continue researching its summoning and banishment."

Pauline nodded. "In general, we all garden organically, but there are some things you don't mess around with—couch grass, bindweed. This is one of those things."

"And you think it'll work?" Katie asked.

Pauline shrugged. "It's worth a try. What's the worst that could happen? It doesn't work, and we try something else."

"Okay." Katie had no better ideas, short of getting a backhoe in to dig them out. And she wasn't convinced that digging them out would kill them.

The women returned an hour later with a backpack sprayer, and Katie crossed her fingers hoping that was the end of her troubles.

# Chapter 16

## *Multiplying Monsters*

It wasn't.

Three 'drunks' got into a fight in the car park Saturday night, despite no alcohol being consumed on the premises. Thankfully, the police didn't get involved. Katie hoped the neighbours hadn't noticed the ruckus.

The only bright spot on Saturday evening was that Finn returned. Katie couldn't help smiling when he walked in. "This isn't your night," she said, intercepting him near the door as she helped clear tables.

Finn shrugged. "Thought you could probably use the business tonight. I enjoyed that mocktail last night."

He came just to support her business? "Aw, that's really sweet. Taine's bartending again this evening. Pull up a stool."

"I was kinda thinking I'd sit at a table. Have a meal, you know?"

"A meal?" Katie's smile widened and she waved a hand around the dining room. "There are plenty of empty tables. Have a seat, and I'll bring you a menu."

Heading back to the bar to snag a menu, Katie passed Tui. "He's getting a meal," she sang in her friend's ear.

Tui squealed. "Next he'll be asking you out. Go get him, girl!"

Katie dropped off a menu at Finn's table. "Can I get you something to drink?"

He smiled up at her. "Same as last night?"

"You bet." Katie was about to turn away, when Finn stopped her.

"Hey, um ... I was talking to a friend who lives in Rifton earlier today. I hope it's okay, I mentioned your problem. With the drunks and your liquor licence."

Great. Just what she needed—someone broadcasting the fact she'd lost her licence. The bubble of pleasure at seeing Finn burst and her smile vanished. "Yeah?"

Finn raised his hands at her tone of voice. "He already knew you'd lost your licence. Honestly, I suspect everyone in Rifton heard about it within an hour of you opening yesterday."

Katie's heart sank to her toes. Great.

Finn continued. "My friend *was* surprised at why you lost your licence. There was never trouble with behaviour in the car park with the old pub, and he says there were a *lot* of people leaving that place drunk every Saturday night."

"Did he have any clues as to why people who haven't had a single drink are acting intoxicated in the car park now?" Katie asked.

"He had no clue, but he did suggest you talk to the Rifton garden group. Apparently one of the women in the group used to own the pub, and he said there are rumours of strange things happening here over the years. Maybe they know something?" Finn shrugged.

Well, that was interesting. Katie laughed. "Yeah. I've had a talk with them about the problem."

"And?"

No way in hell was she going to tell him what they had to say about the plants causing the trouble. Hopefully, that rumour wouldn't find its way through the town. "They have some ideas. They're working on it with me."

Finn sat for a moment, eyebrows raised, clearly expecting more details. Time to change the subject.

"So, what will you have?"

Finn glanced down at the menu, then flashed Katie a smile. "Um ... what do you recommend? Obviously, you're not cooking tonight, but are any of these dishes, like, your specialty or something?"

Oh my god, was the man flirting? Her irritation at him talking about her problems with someone else vanished. There was nothing better than a guy asking about her food. "Well, they're all my recipes, although some are pretty standard dishes."

"What about this lamb and minted peas sushi? Are you Japanese?"

Katie chuckled. "No. My grandmother is from China. But I love sushi. And minted peas. I liked the idea of Kiwi-Asian fusion."

"Sounds good. I'll have that, please." He handed the menu back to her, holding her gaze for a moment. He *was* flirting. It felt ... good.

Katie all but skipped back to the bar. At the moment, she didn't feel like a struggling new business owner. She forgot all her responsibilities and worries beyond ordering Finn's drink and food, and making sure it arrived at his table looking and tasting amazing.

"You have a goofy smile on your face, girl," Tui said. "He ask you out?"

"Not yet. But he ordered my lamb and pea sushi."

"Did you tell him it was your invention?"

"He asked which one was my signature dish."

"Hot damn!"

"That's what I thought too."

Her elation had lasted only as long as Finn's meal. He didn't ask her out, and shortly after he left, a fight broke out in the car park.

As she fell asleep that night, she replayed the day in her head. Had it really started out with a bunch of women meeting to discuss the demons in her car park? Before her brain got stuck on the demon/liquor licence conundrum, she forced herself to focus on Finn. Back at uni, she and Tui had always challenged each other to get guys to ask them out. Sure, women could do the asking, but there was something rewarding about being asked. And it was even better if you had to work to get the guy to do it—the thrill of the chase and all. Did she want Finn to ask her out? Did she have *time* to go on a date, even if he did ask? Was she absolutely certain he wasn't the cause of the trouble at The Tipsy Teapot? She didn't have definitive answers to any of those questions, although she was reasonably certain he wasn't trying to sabotage her.

When she'd argued to Tui that she couldn't go on a date because she worked all the time, Tui had barked at her. "You've created this workplace where your employees can get time off and don't have to live in fear of losing their jobs if they're sick or need to take a personal day. Why are you acting like you're still working at Brennan's? You've left that cutthroat scene behind. All of your employees are enjoying it, why won't you cut yourself some slack? You're the *owner*—you can do whatever the hell you want."

"But there's so much to do. And I don't want to let you all down by shirking my duties."

Tui had snorted. "Yeah, like we all think you're a slacker, the way you step in and do jobs whenever needed, even though you could easily order one of us to do it. The way you immediately jump on any little problem and fix it. Katie, your kitchen runs more smoothly, and more humanely, than any other place I've worked, and it's because of all the hard work you put into it. You can take a break for an evening to go on a date."

"And what if he *is* the one responsible for me losing my liquor licence? I can't be dating him!"

Tui had waved a hand. "He's not. Sorry I ever suggested that. It's clear he's into you."

In front of Tui, Katie had dismissed the idea that Finn was into her, but part of her wanted to believe he was. Maybe she could date the man. No. She *would*. And she'd get Finn to do the asking—she was going to enjoy the challenge.

With that pleasant thought, she drifted off to sleep, looking forward to tomorrow.

Katie's optimism lasted only until she arrived at The Tipsy Teapot Sunday morning. She rounded the corner, glanced into the car park, and sucked in a breath.

*Shit!*

She rang Alex, though it was only six-thirty in the morning.

"Hello?" Alex's voice was thick with sleep, and Katie winced. She'd have to take some yummy baked goods to her later to make up for this.

"Alex, I'm so sorry to wake you. I just got to work and ... it looks like the herbicide didn't work."

"I think it takes a few days for the stuff to take effect. You might not see a difference this morning," Alex replied with a yawn.

"Oh, there's a difference. A big one. The demon plants have doubled in size overnight, and there are little bright green seedlings sprouting at the base of every plant."

Alex swore, and her next words bore no trace of sleepiness. "I'm on my way. See you in five minutes. Don't go near the plants."

*As if.* Katie ran her finger over the scratches on her neck from the other day. They were still itchy and red.

Alex arrived, dragging a yawning Shel through the door, just as Katie slipped the first trays of pastries into the ovens. Jill had Sundays off, but she prepared a range of items on Saturday and left them in the fridge for Katie to bake in the morning.

"Twenty minutes to fresh raspberry muffins," Katie announced. "Have a seat. Coffee?"

"Yes please," they answered in unison.

Katie began fixing coffees. "I assume you had a look at the plants on your way in?"

"We did," Alex said. "And I rang Margaret, from the garden group. She's mustering the troops. They should be here shortly."

"What? All of them? At this hour?"

Alex laughed. "If they're anything like my gran was, they've been up for hours already."

Katie carried a tray of coffees to the table where Alex and Shel sat. "Sorry to get you both out of bed. I suppose it could have waited."

Shel waved away her apology. "No worries. If I had woken to that scene out there, I'd have rung Alex, too."

Alex slapped him lightly on the arm. "Hey, this one's not my fault."

"Yeah, but you're braver than I am."

"I don't know. I may just be dumber than you." Alex held

out her hand, revealing a fresh scratch along her palm. "Like an idiot, I tried to pull out one of the seedlings."

"After you told *me* not to touch them," Katie said, raising her eyebrows.

"Well, they're little. It might have worked."

Katie sipped her coffee. "I'm thinking of hiring a contractor to dig them out with a backhoe."

"Oh, that's a good idea," Alex said.

"Until the backhoe operator starts noticing the plants are fighting back," Shel said. "And how do we know pulling them out of the soil will kill them? We have to stop thinking of them as plants."

"But isn't it worth *trying*?" Katie was trying not to freak out. "We can't cut them, and herbicide is apparently like fertiliser to them … If I can't get rid of them, I'm going to have to shut my business."

"Not to mention what happens when they spread beyond your car park." Alex's voice was grim.

"Maybe we could dig one of the seedlings out with a shovel as a test—if we can kill a little one by digging it out, then we can maybe hire a digger." Shel smiled. "I've always wanted to drive one of those things, and it would avoid any awkward questions from a contractor."

Katie perked up. "I've got a shovel in the wee shed out the back."

Alex slammed back the last of her coffee. "Let's give it a go."

They collected the shovel, and Katie dug out a pair of gumboots some guy had forgotten at the pub a couple of weeks ago.

Shel handed the shovel to Alex. "Your sword, oh brave one."

Alex rolled her eyes. "Fine. I'll do it."

"No," Katie said. "This is *my* problem. I'll do it." She slipped her feet into the gumboots, which were way too large for her, and clomped over to the nearest seedling, choosing one as far from an adult plant as possible.

She set the tip of the spade on the soil close to the seedling and pressed it in. It didn't go far, and Alex called out a warning as all the plants—demons—nearby started swaying in agitation. Katie stomped on the back of the shovel, driving it fully into the soil, and then she levered the seedling out with a clump of dirt. Stepping further from the thrashing plants, Katie dumped the seedling on the ground, knocked the clinging soil off its roots, and then flicked it onto the pavement of the car park. All the while, the little seedling twisted and shook, 'biting' at the shovel with its little leaves.

Katie swallowed. The thing was *sentient*. How could that be? She took a step back, her heart thrashing wildly in her chest.

The seedling wiggled and thrashed, roots and leaves flailing on the pavement. It shoved itself upright, roots steadying it like long toes. It swayed for a moment, as if getting its bearings, and then scuttled towards Katie.

She screeched, dropped the shovel and staggered backwards. She'd never had a panic attack, but now felt like the appropriate time for one.

Alex swooped in, picked up the shovel and brought it down with a clang on top of the seedling. Ruthlessly, she hit it again and again. Katie wasn't sure which was more disturbing, the scuttling sentient plant or Alex beating it senseless with a shovel.

"It won't work." The voice behind Katie made her jump. Across the car park strode the members of the garden group. They were kitted out with gloves, boots and sun hats. Each brandished a long-handled lopper or, inexplicably, a butterfly net.

"You won't kill a demon with a shovel," Pauline said.

Alex straightened, shovel poised. "Look. It's not moving anymore."

She'd barely finished speaking when the demon picked itself up and scuttled away, tucking itself under the branches of one of the mature plants and wiggling its roots back into the soil.

Alex's shoulders slumped. "Yeah, I figured it wouldn't work, but it felt good."

Katie gestured to the older women's tools. "What do you have in mind?"

"Well, first I suppose we need to apologise," Jane said. "I wasn't convinced the herbicide would kill them, but this?" She waved a hand at the lush, newly grown greenery. "None of us expected it to act like a growth hormone."

The other women murmured their agreement and apologies. Katie waved her hand. "You see how well *my* idea worked. I thought the herbicide was a good idea, too."

"We thought today we should try some containment," Margaret said, pulling a large glass jar out of a tote bag slung over her shoulder. "We're still trying to find a way to banish or destroy them, but we decided we should cut off flowers and collect seeds if we can. Keep the little beggars from reproducing."

Alex nodded. "Make sure they don't spread further."

Katie brightened. "And if we take off the flowers, maybe they won't be able to intoxicate my customers. I should have thought of that before."

Shel looked dubious. "You think you'll be able to cut the flowers?"

Margaret grinned. "We won't know until we try."

# Chapter 17

## *Botane dubia*

"What do you need us to do?" Katie asked.

"Just step back and let us work," Pauline said.

"And keep an eye on the plants we're not focused on. Warn us if they do anything ... odd," Sharon said as she adjusted her gloves.

Odd, as in picking themselves up and walking away after being pounded with a shovel? Katie rubbed her temples. What the hell was going on here? She still wasn't certain she entirely understood or believed what she'd seen with her own eyes. But the presence of the armed garden group was oddly reassuring.

The women moved with the precision of a military unit as Pauline barked directions. "Sharon, you're with me. We'll start on the plant on the left. Ellen and Jane, take the one next to ours. Margaret, is the jar ready? Keep the lid on unless we're dropping something in. Do your best to stay out of the way of the branches. Ready?"

The others nodded.

"Let's go."

Sharon and Pauline advanced quickly, in tandem with Ellen and Jane, while Margaret waited with the jar. Stretching her loppers to the closest dangling flower, Pauline deftly snapped the blades shut around the stem. Sharon held her net below the bloom to catch it as it fell.

Except it didn't fall.

The plant writhed and thrashed, beating at the loppers. Pauline frowned and snapped the blades open and shut again. Again the bloom failed to fall. Sharon's net was being buffeted by branches, and Katie wasn't sure she would have caught the flower even had it fallen.

At the next plant, a similar scene was playing out. Ellen yelped as the plant grabbed her loppers and yanked, jerking her forward until she lost her grip. The loppers disappeared into the foliage, and then a series of loud snapping sounds reverberated around the car park. A moment later fragments of metal and splinters of wood shot out of the plant. Jane dropped her net, and both she and Ellen covered their heads as debris from the loppers rained down on them.

Pauline yanked her loppers back, shouting, "Retreat!"

Jane snatched her net up as a plant reached for it. Everyone staggered backwards. Next to Katie, Pauline was breathing hard. She raised her loppers and examined the notched and bent blades. "Damn. They were a nice pair of loppers."

"It shredded my net!" Sharon stared at the wisps of netting fluttering from the net's bent wire rim.

"Well, it was worth a try," Alex said.

Movement behind Alex caught Katie's eye. Terror shot through her. "Alex!" she screeched, pointing.

Alex turned, raising the shovel she still held, as one of the larger demonic plants tore itself from the soil and stalked on writhing roots towards them.

Shel swore and everyone focused on the plants as, one by one, the larger ones pulled their roots up and began to advance. Dirt flew off their roots and skittered across the pavement. Branches thrashed, and the crab-claw leaves snapped angrily.

"Now what?" Katie squeaked. Those creatures had snapped her broom and chewed up a pair of loppers—the party's collective weapons of a shovel, two insect nets, and the remaining twisted loppers seemed woefully inadequate. Still, Katie wished she had her broom.

The plants advanced quickly.

"Form up!" Pauline barked, and they closed ranks, facing the plants.

Katie's heart thrashed in her chest. "We should run for it. We can't fight them off."

Alex shook her head. "Something tells me they're a lot faster than they look. I'm not turning my back on them."

"They're predators," Margaret said. "All we have to do is show them we're not worth the effort to kill."

Katie had the sinking feeling that this was not about predation anymore—it was about revenge.

The demonic plants closed in on them. Alex swung at them with her shovel and missed. Pauline snapped her loppers threateningly.

Katie took a step backwards. Something sharp stabbed her in the ankle. She yelped and looked down. Dozens of little demonic plants swarmed behind them. They'd circled around while the humans were all focused on the big plants.

"Ouch!" Shel swore as one of the baby plants nipped his ankle. "Shit. Watch your feet!"

The instant the weapon-wielders' focus switched to the little plants swarming their ankles, the big ones pounced.

Alex swung her shovel, and the crunch of metal on branches rang out across the car park. Margaret hurled her jar at a plant slashing towards her face. The jar clattered into the branches, and then smashed on the pavement. Jane lunged with her net, stabbing the trunk of the plant in front of her. Katie heard the snap of wood as the plant broke the net handle.

Then her focus was drawn to her feet, where another bite seared into her ankle. With a growl, she shook the seedling off and stomped on it. The stunned plant was still for a moment, and Katie stomped on another advancing on her. Anger swelled to overcome her fear. How dare these plants threaten her, threaten her business and her new friends! Whoever had brought them here was going to pay for it. She imagined each one of the seedlings was the person who was trying to sabotage her business. *Stomp. Stomp. Stomp. Take that, you arsehole!*

But a stomp only stunned the plants, and they kept coming. Katie had no time to see how the others were faring, but the grunts and curses, the snaps, clangs and bashes resounding around her told her they were in trouble.

Alex gave a yelp, and an object streaked by Katie's head. She looked up in time to see the shovel fly halfway across the car park and clang to the ground, twisted and bent, with a splintered handle.

Fear took hold again, and Katie stomped frantically at the snapping plants. She dared a glance at her companions.

Alex was grappling with the plant in front of her. Pauline still wielded her loppers, but they were even more twisted than before. Sharon and Jane each clutched the splintered remnants of their nets, jabbing them at the slashing branches. Margaret, Ellen and Shel frantically stomped seedlings, defending everyone's ankles.

"What do we do?" Katie screamed, kicking at an approaching seedling. There was no way they could fight these things off much longer.

"Can we make a break for the pub?" Shel asked.

Margaret's voice was breathless. "Depends on how fast

they are."

"We can't hold out much longer," Jane cried as the last remaining splinters of her net were snatched from her hand.

"Right. On the count of three, we run," Pauline said. "One ... two ..."

"Katie? Shit! Katie!" The familiar voice of Aunt Rachael rang out across the car park. Katie glanced up to see Rachael breaking into a run as she fumbled in her purse.

A seedling bit Katie's toe, and she focused on her feet again. Rachael's heels pounded across the pavement, growing closer.

"Rachael, stay back!" Katie yelled. "These things are—"

"Demons. I know." Aunt Rachael joined the fray armed with a small spray bottle. *Psht!* A mist settled on the demons at Katie's feet, and the plants squealed and recoiled. *Psht! Psht! Psht!* Rachael descended on the demons like some avenging angel with bubblegum-pink hair, purple lipstick, a fuchsia top and purple stilettos to match. Every squirt of her bottle sent a demon into fits of squealing. In moments, the seedlings were all scurrying towards the shelter of the larger plants. When Rachael turned her spray to the adult plants, they recoiled. Alex released her grip on the plant in front of her—or maybe it released its grip on *her*, Katie wasn't sure—and staggered backwards, covered in bleeding scratches.

Rachael advanced, spraying the plants with calm ruthlessness. Slowly they backed away from her. When they broke ranks and scurried back to the edge of the car park and sank their roots back into the soil, Rachael gave a satisfied nod. "And stay the fuck over there," she called to them.

Rachael turned to the dishevelled and bleeding group and whipped off her sunglasses. "Whew! Good thing I had a new bottle of this in my purse." She tossed the spray bottle into the air and caught it with a grin. "A minute longer and I would have run out."

The others must have been as stunned as Katie was, because they all stared wordlessly at Aunt Rachael.

"Katie-pie! It's so good to see you. The pub looks *amazing*! You should be proud." Aunt Rachael gave Katie an appraising look, and then frowned. "But what the fuck are you doing with *Botane dubia*?"

Katie cleared her throat. "With what?" Did Rachael recognise the plant?

"*Botane dubia*, also known as exhortation plant or compulsion plant. It's—" Rachael's eyes darted around the group.

"We know it's not a plant," Alex said.

Margaret piped up. "My familiar says it's a demon, but that's all he knows. If you can tell us more, we'd all appreciate it, especially your niece."

Rachael's eyes grew even wider. "You have a familiar?" Her smile returned. "Oh, this is even better than I'd hoped!"

What the hell was she talking about? "Rachael, did *you* do this?" She waved a hand at the demonic plants, anger rising in her chest. "Because these things have cost me my liquor licence."

Rachael raised her hands. "No way. I would never summon these things."

Summon. Not plant, grow, or sow. "Well how do you know about them then? And what did you spray on them?"

Rachael laughed. "Sunblock. Who would have thought?"

"You mean you didn't know it would work?" Pauline asked.

"Had no idea. Lucky guess. It was either that or hand sanitiser." Rachael turned her attention back to Katie. "We should talk."

*Yeah, no shit.*

"And you should introduce me to your friends." Rachael's eyes glittered. "I think I'm going to like them."

After introductions, Katie invited them all into the pub. She pulled out the first-aid kit, and sent everyone to the upstairs toilets to clean up and bandage their wounds. No one was badly hurt, but those demon bites were painful and itchy. Katie rubbed at her ankles, thankful her socks and pants had offered some protection against the bites.

Katie's weekend chef, Xavier, was due to arrive shortly, and her other staff wouldn't be far behind, so Katie suggested they chat in the upstairs function room where they would have privacy.

Xavier arrived as she was lifting a tray of coffees to take upstairs. "Hey Katie. Wow. That's quite a coffee fix," he said, eyeing the tray. Then his eyes flicked to her face. "You look awful. Is everything alright?"

Katie gave a mirthless laugh. "Yeah. I'm up in the conference room with some folks. We're dealing with a ... a bit of a situation." Xavier frowned, and Katie quickly tried to quash his curiosity. "Nothing you need to worry about, but I won't be able to help out for a while. And I haven't put the scones in the oven yet."

"No worries. Sunday mornings start slow. I'll deal with the scones. We'll be fine."

"Thanks. And I hate to ask, but can you prep three teas and bring up a selection of baked goods for us? The muffins and cinnamon scrolls are on the cooling racks. Oh, and better bring up a couple of pieces of carrot cake."

"Sure thing. How many of you?"

"Nine." Katie started towards the stairs as Xavier grabbed another tray and got to work.

At the top of the steps, she was surprised to find everyone gathered around the entrance to the store room. "Um ...guys

... the conference room is here." The door was open—it was obvious where they were meant to go.

"We know. But I wanted to see the storeroom," Aunt Rachael said.

What? Katie ducked into the conference room and deposited the tray on the table. Returning to the hallway, she asked, "Why do you want to see the storeroom?"

It was Margaret who answered. "This was Room Four. It's where the fire started, and it ... well, the room has a reputation."

"Reputation?" Katie remembered Margaret suggesting using Room Four as a storeroom because of the potential for a lingering smoke smell. Was there a different reason she didn't think it should be part of the conference room?

"Liz and Simon Harris owned the pub from around 1980 to the early two-thousands. Liz was in the garden group, and she told some strange stories about this room," Margaret said.

Sharon continued the tale. "There was once an infestation of bed bugs the size of German shepherds." She added air quotes around the words bed bugs.

"People would come to the pub and specifically request Room Four," Pauline added.

"And Thunder, the pub cat, was absolutely obsessed with the room and anyone staying in it," Margaret concluded.

Alex and Shel's eyes widened, and Alex leaned forward. "The pub cat was Thunder? Gran's cat Thunder? Was he a—"

Margaret nodded. "We don't know for certain, but there are stories of a large grey cat living at the pub since the early nineteen-hundreds. We think it's the same cat, or rather, demon. But we don't know who might have summoned it or why."

Katie frowned and turned to Alex. "Isn't your gran's cat black?"

"She had two cats, Thor, whom you've met, and Thunder, a grey cat."

Shel spoke up. "Thunder helped us banish the materpodas—those giant centipedes we told you about. He picked up one of the babies and carried it through the portal. Vanished along with the materpodas."

The creaking of steps warned that Xavier was coming up with tea and muffins. Without a word they all filed into the conference room. Xavier set the tray in the middle of the conference table.

"Oh! Dibs on the carrot cake," Sharon said.

"Yeah? Is it good?" Aunt Rachael asked, reaching for a piece.

"Try it and see for yourself."

Katie waited until Xavier had gone back downstairs and everyone was comfortably settled with a drink and a muffin before bombarding Rachael with questions. "Okay, Aunt Rachael. Spill. What the hell is going on? How do you know what those plant-demon things are? What was that comment you made about Margaret's familiar? And why didn't you tell me about those demons when you gave me this fecking pub?"

Rachael took a bite of her cake. "Mmm. That's good." She chewed for a moment. "The icing—" Katie flung a scowl at her aunt across the table, and Rachael sighed. "I've been studying witchcraft for ... well, most of my adult life. Did you know one of our ancestors was a *wu*—a shaman? Xue Liu— she would have been your great-great-grandmother. Anyway, I did a project on genealogy in high school, and was intrigued by her story. I started looking into shamanism, and then got interested in other cultures' witchcraft traditions. I mix and match practices and traditions from lots of cultures."

"So you're a witch?" The idea illuminated a great deal about Katie's wacky aunt.

Rachael laughed. "You don't have to say it like it's a disease. Anyway, I'd heard rumours about the town of Rifton. Chatted with an old woman once who swore the veil between the spirit world and our world was torn here. Made it easier to travel between worlds, easier to summon demons. So when the pub came up for sale, I knew I had to buy it for you, just so I'd have an excuse to come to Rifton."

Alex and Shel glanced at each other knowingly. "That would explain a few things," Alex said.

"Oh?" replied Rachael. "Have you summoned a demon?"

"Not on purpose."

Margaret leaned forward. "But her grandmother and I each summoned a *Felis daemonicus,* and we believe that until recently there was another demonic cat in Rifton—the pub cat, Thunder."

"Who summoned the compulsion plants?" Rachael asked.

"We don't know," Jane said.

"They appeared, pretty much overnight, shortly after I started renovations," Katie explained.

Rachael frowned in thought. "And I can imagine how they've led to the loss of your liquor licence."

"You can?" How much did Aunt Rachael know about these things?

Her aunt nodded. "It's called compulsion plant because the perfume of its flowers makes people suggestible. A person will do anything anyone even vaguely suggests while under the influence of that smell. You've had a lot of trouble with 'drunks', haven't you?"

"Every night, and most of them hadn't had more than one drink. We've figured out it was the plants—demons—doing it. We just haven't been able to get rid of them," Katie explained. "And now they've reproduced!"

"Do you know how to do a banishment?" Aunt Rachael asked.

"Rachael, I don't even know what a banishment is! This demon stuff is all nonsense to me."

Shel leaned forward. "Alex and I have done one. We know how. More or less."

Rachael nodded. "Good. I'm certain I have the summoning spell for *Botaneȝ dubia*. I'll email it to Katie when I get home later today."

"Do you know the flicker pattern we need?" Shel asked.

"Flicker pattern?" Rachael's eyebrows rose.

"A summoning, or a banishment, requires flickering light, in addition to the spoken words."

"That's why you're supposed to put candles around your summoning circle, right?"

Shel nodded. "Yes, but what Alex and I discovered is that there is a precise flicker pattern needed to make the incantation work. Apparently, it's not critical to get it perfect for the summoning, but the banishment is trickier."

Rachael's eyes lit up. "Really? I've never heard that."

Alex snorted. "Yeah, we didn't use candles. We used fairy lights and an app on my phone that made them flicker to the beat of a song. The song we used was based on some tapping patterns the materpoda made—a lucky choice. I assume that each demon requires a different flicker pattern, just like each requires a different incantation."

"But we don't know that for certain," Shel added. "We just know what worked for the materpoda."

"Well you know more than I do about that, then," Rachael replied. "I'll send you the spell. That's the most I can do for you."

"Thank you. It's a lot more than we have at the moment," Alex said gratefully. Then she turned to Katie. "Shel and I will watch the plants closely today, see if we can discern a rhythm we can use."

Katie was a bit overwhelmed. "Okay. If you know what to do, great. But are you sure it's safe to get close to them again?"

Alex barked a laugh. "No. But we're going to have to do so in order to get rid of them."

# Interlude 6

## *2020*

Derrick slotted the key into the lock of Room Four. His nose wrinkled at the musty smell that hit him as he pushed open the door. This place was a pit. Did he really have to do this ... this summoning ... *here*? What was so special about this particular disgusting old pub hotel and this particular room?

There was nothing obviously special about the room, unless you considered cheap laminate furniture special. He supposed he should be thankful there was no carpet on the old wooden floor—no doubt it would have been mouldy. Black mildew spotted the lace curtains, and he threw open the window to try to dispel some of the mouldy smell.

Well, the old woman was adamant he do this in the Rifton Pub, in Room Four, but he didn't have to stay the night here. He'd do what he needed to, then head to a nice hotel. Colette didn't expect him home until Thursday. No doubt she was on another bender without him there to keep her in check. It didn't really matter when he got home.

He carefully shut the door and locked it. He lifted his almost empty suitcase to the bed and opened it, pulling out a single sheet of paper on which was written a set of instructions in a shaky hand.

He reviewed the first three numbered points, and then pulled a box of chalk, purchased that morning at a bookshop in Christchurch, from the suitcase. Now the bare floor made more sense—the old woman had said to draw a chalk circle on it. He eyed the space. There wasn't a lot of room. She said the demon would manifest inside the circle. How big would the thing be? He'd counted on bringing it home in his suitcase, so it better not be too large.

He laughed. Was he actually going to try this? He wasn't even sure he believed in magic, and here he was in a seedy hotel room preparing to summon a demon. Damn. He must seriously be desperate.

Well, he was. He'd pinned all his hopes on Colette when he'd married her. She was the perfect wife—rich and supportive of the arts. And he'd been her perfect husband—a handsome young struggling author. At least that's what he told her. In truth, he had no intention of ever writing the book he claimed to be writing—the magnificent tale full of angst, drama, and deep environmental themes that so captivated Colette's imagination.

That he wasn't upholding his end of the deal didn't negate his dismay at Colette's squandering of her fortune. Her alcohol and drug use had been recreational at first, but now it was all-consuming. Derrick's dream of easy living was flowing down the drain as Colette spent astonishing sums of money on her addictions, and then threw away the rest on ridiculous causes while under the influence.

It had to stop. Like a dutiful spouse, he'd suggested

treatment, but she refused to admit she had a problem. If he didn't act soon, he'd be forced to actually work for a living. He reckoned his options were either to collect on her hefty life insurance policy, or divorce her and try to win as much in settlement as possible.

As self-destructive as she was, Colette was unlikely to die before she ran through her money. Derrick would have to do the deed if he wanted the life insurance money. The thought made him queasy. He was a scoundrel, no doubt, and he wasn't in love with his wife. But he was not a murderer.

That left divorce. His mate Zach was a lawyer, and he'd actually laughed in Derrick's face when he asked if he could clean out Colette in a divorce settlement. "Have you been caring for children? Volunteering in the family business? Doing anything of note for the good of the household? Dude, a judge is going to look at you and tell you to get a job. The best you can hope for is a year or two of maintenance while you get your shit together."

So he needed to convince Colette to hand over her money in the divorce without going to court. He'd floated the idea of handing over finances to him when he discussed her drug use, but she insisted she was fine and didn't need a financial babysitter.

All the while, she was draining her bank accounts.

That was when he turned to Mrs Henderson, their house cleaner. She was a short woman who wore her long grey hair tightly coiled into a bun. She had piercing green eyes and wrinkles like plough furrows all over her face. She was also a witch.

Derrick knew this, because she liked to chat while she worked, and he was often home when she arrived on a Thursday morning. He liked her, even if she was an odd bat. She'd helped him once or twice before for minor things—she'd given him a cure for acid reflux (which he'd requested), and an aphrodisiac (which he hadn't asked for, but she somehow deduced the need).

He had initially baulked at her suggestion of summoning a demon, even if the thing was called compulsion plant. He'd been hoping for a simple potion to slip into Colette's liquor. Maybe Mrs Henderson had worked out why he wanted to make someone agree to his demands. After Derrick cleaned Colette out with a divorce settlement and moved to Fiji, Mrs Henderson would lose her job. Maybe by suggesting the demon, she was hoping to dissuade him from his plan. Of course, the woman would lose her job sooner or later, when Colette ran out of money.

At first, he was dissuaded. But the more he thought about it, the more he liked the idea of having a demon plant that could convince people to do his bidding. It could come in handy, even after the divorce. The idea of a life in which he simply had to ask someone for what he wanted and it was handed over was quite appealing.

So here he was, in this godforsaken pub in the backwater of Rifton, drawing a pentagram on the floor and placing candles at the points of the star.

He stood back and surveyed his work. The star was wonky, but at least the circle was pretty good. How accurate did he need to be? Mrs Henderson hadn't said.

He picked up the instructions again and read the next step. *Open a window. The best results are obtained with a lively breeze entering the room.* He shook his head. He didn't understand why a breeze was important, but he'd already opened the window, so that was good. He continued reading. *Light the candles in an anticlockwise fashion, beginning with the candle on the northern edge of the pentagram.* What the hell direction was north? He pulled out his phone and oriented himself on a map. Determining the northernmost candle, he pulled a lighter from his pocket and lit all five candles. The flames danced in the breeze. What happened if one blew out? Did he have to extinguish them all and relight them in the correct order? The instructions didn't say.

*Say the following incantation aloud while standing inside your circle.* He had to stand inside it? Wasn't the demon going to materialise there? The thought made him uneasy. Maybe he should have clarified a few more details with Mrs Henderson before he'd come.

Oh well, he was here now. He stepped into the circle and began to read.

"Leafy splendour, hither come. Though by thy nature deaf and dumb, hear my voice. Heed my call. Into the portal deftly fall. Compelling creature be compelled. Come to me and be bespelled."

He laughed. What ridiculous nonsense. Was something supposed to happen when he said the words? He scanned further down the instructions.

*Summonings are difficult. Do not expect to succeed on the first try. You may want to adjust the window so that the breeze is lively, but not excessive. Ensure that all candles remain lit. Speak clearly.*

Okay. Derrick cleared his throat and read the summoning again.

Nothing happened.

Was the breeze too lively? Too weak? He pushed the window open further, glancing down to the car park below as a laughing group of people exited the pub and drifted to their cars.

Returning to the circle, he appraised the candles. Still burning, guttering and flickering a bit more now. He hoped the breeze wouldn't blow them out. He stepped into the circle and read the incantation again.

As the last syllable of 'bespelled' left his lips, a crack and flash like lightning sent him cowering to his knees, hands over his head. Cracking open one eye, he saw a gnarled root writhing next to his knee. With a yelp, he jumped up, stepping out of the circle, heart pounding.

A creature stood in the centre of the circle. Had Derrick seen it in a garden, he would have dismissed it as some ornamental plant, but standing in the middle of a bare wood floor, its rootlike feet slithering like knobby snakes along the boards, there was no mistaking it for a plant. Its 'leaves' bore serrated edges, and it snapped them together like crab claws. Large red flowers dangled from arching branches. They would have been attractive had they not been jiggling wildly with the scrabbling motion of the branches. Their sickly sweet stench quickly permeated the room, and Derrick was reminded of the smell of honeysuckle on his mum's back fence.

Then another smell broke through Derrick's breathless examination of the demon. Smoke.

He glanced down to find his sheet of instructions in flames. It must have fallen out of his hand when the demon appeared, and it had come to rest against one of the candles. Now it was quickly turning to ash.

"No!" Derrick lunged for the paper and frantically waved it about to extinguish the flames. "Shit!" He needed those instructions. What was he supposed to do next? How was he supposed to get this creature, at least a metre tall, into his suitcase? He peered at the page, its blackened edges flaking in his trembling hands. Nearly a third of the page was gone. The remaining steps Mrs Henderson had written out for him had been almost entirely consumed.

*Once the demon is ... wait for a minu ... return the creature ...*

It was useless. The scraps of writing that remained made no sense. He'd have to figure it out on his own.

He rubbed his sweaty palms on his pants and willed his breathing to steady. *Think.* He needed to somehow get the demon into the suitcase. It might fit, with a little bending and squishing.

The circle would contain the demon—he remembered that much from what Mrs Henderson had told him. So he should bring the suitcase into the circle, to avoid accidentally letting it loose in the room. Who knew how fast the thing moved, but he didn't fancy chasing it around.

He picked up the suitcase and stood just outside the circle, clutching it to his chest. Could he clap it over the top of the demon, squish it down and zip it up, without having to touch the beast? Unlikely. It would take some careful bending to fit it in, especially the roots, which seemed to be lengthening as he watched, questing around the circle. He shuddered. Maybe this was a bad idea.

He thought of Colette's fortune—*his* fortune—and how she was drinking and snorting it away while he stood here dithering.

Before he could lose the nerve, he stepped into the circle. The demon's 'branches' waved more frantically, leaves snapping in his direction. He set down the suitcase.

"Relax there, mate. I'm not going to hurt you," he said in what he hoped was a soothing tone. "We're just going to get you into the bag, and then I'll take you to a nice new home." He'd originally planned to give the demon to Colette as a potted plant, to set next to her favourite recliner. But now he was thinking he'd plant it in the ground next to the deck where Colette sat and vaped every morning. "You'll have a nice garden all to yourself," he continued, reaching out towards the creature's trunk. The branches waved. Flowers danced near Derrick's face, and he wrinkled his nose at the cloying floral scent. Then he lunged, grabbing the trunk and tipping the demon over into the suitcase.

Branches flailed in Derrick's face, and a root lashed his side. He had the thing on its side, but if he couldn't get it to stay still, he'd never get it zipped into the suitcase.

A root curled into a ball like a fist and punched him in the stomach. Derrick let out a grunt. Then a pair of snipping leaves crunched down on his forearm, and Derrick bit back a scream. He let go of the demon and staggered back, out of the circle, clutching at his arm and cursing.

Deep gashes on his arm bled profusely, like he'd been attacked with a pair of scissors. Derrick pressed the hem of his shirt on the wounds. The demon blundered out of the suitcase and back upright, leaves snapping angrily. It wrapped a root around the handle of the suitcase and hurled it across the room. The suitcase banged against the wall, then thumped to the floor. The demon began to shuffle around the circle, probing it with its roots, as though searching for a way out. Derrick scanned the chalk line to make sure it was still intact before snatching up the pair of boxers he'd brought for tomorrow and using them as a bandage on his arm.

The steps outside creaked as someone ascended. He desperately tried to calm his breathing. Shit. Had someone heard him?

There was a knock on the door. "Mr Boone? Everything okay in here?" It was the woman from the bar downstairs, who had checked him in.

"Yeah, all good, thanks!" he called, trying and failing to inject a hearty note into his voice.

"It's just, I heard a lot of banging."

"Oh, yeah. Clumsy me dropped my suitcase on the floor. Everything's fine." *Go away, lady.*

"Okay, well, if you need anything, pop on down. You can either eat in the restaurant, or I can bring up anything on the menu for you."

"Great. Thanks!"

Derrick breathed a sigh of relief as he heard the woman's footsteps retreat back down the stairs.

Now what was he going to do? This demon wouldn't fit in his suitcase, even if it didn't try to kill him when he approached it. How was he going to get it home?

He began to pace, then stopped himself—the woman downstairs would hear him. She might come back up.

Could he tie a rope, like a leash, to it and lead it out to his car? It would fit in the boot, if he could get it there. He laughed. It hadn't shown any sign of being docile or compliant, and how would he avoid being seen leading a walking shrubbery out of the pub?

*Shit, shit, shit.* What was he supposed to do? He sank down onto the bed, sitting on the edge and rubbing his face with his uninjured hand.

*Shuffle. Shuffle. Shuffle.* The demon scraped along the floor. What if he wrapped it in a sheet or something? Immobilised it so it couldn't bite or thrash around. Those scissor-like leaves would be able to snip through it, but it might work long enough to get the thing to the car.

He stood and tossed aside the pillow and duvet. He stripped the sheet off the bed, then replaced the duvet and pillow. When he left, he didn't want things to look amiss.

He eyed up the demon and held the sheet up, planning how he would toss it over the creature, then tie the corners together to secure it. He gave it an experimental flick, tossing it towards a wooden chair next to the bed to see how it moved when he threw it.

It mostly missed the chair, billowing away from it and slithering to the floor. This would take a little practice.

But that was fine. He'd have to wait until quite late to carry the thing out, as the bar didn't close until eleven. He had time to practice.

He tossed the sheet again. Slightly better. It covered the chair, but it wasn't terribly even. He'd need to do better on the demon. He gathered it up and tried again.

A corner of the sheet flicked outward, towards the demon trapped in the circle. The demon darted out a branch, snagging the sheet and whipping it into the circle before Derrick even realised what was happening. Leaves and branches flashed. There was a terrible grinding, ripping, snipping, and within moments, the sheet lay in shreds around the demon.

Derrick swallowed, staring at the creature. "Okay,

we won't do it that way then."

But how *was* he going to get the thing home? He groaned and collapsed onto the chair. Then he sprang up again. The candles! They'd nearly burnt out. He didn't know if they were necessary at this stage, but he wasn't going to take any chances. No way did he want that thing getting out of the circle. Thankfully he'd brought two sets of candles. He lit the new ones from the sputtering stubs of the old ones while the demon waved menacingly in his direction.

He was beginning to think that Colette's fortune wasn't worth this. What if he simply walked out, leaving the demonic plant here? He could get a divorce, and then find himself some new rich woman. He wasn't quite forty yet, and he looked younger than his age. He could catch himself a new sugar mama. She wouldn't even have to be young and attractive like Colette had been, before the drugs and alcohol took their toll. In fact, he could find someone older. Someone he would substantially outlive. He wasn't averse to carrying on an affair on the side, if need be, to satisfy those urges.

Yes, maybe he'd just slip out and let that nice lady downstairs take care of this demon. He lifted the suitcase back to the bed and gathered up the few things he'd brought with him, zipping them inside.

From the open window he could hear a merry group of revellers leaving the pub, singing the old song, 'Light My Fire'. It was horrendously out of tune, and punctuated with laughter, but Derrick's head shot up.

"Light my fire. Light my fire! Of course. That's the solution." It was so obvious, he couldn't believe he hadn't thought of it before. He'd burn that demon to ashes, and that would be that. He opened the drawer of the bedside table and gave a cry of triumph. A Bible. Just the thing. He opened it and began ripping pages out. When he had a good pile of crumpled paper, he dragged over the oil heater, tipped it on its side and removed the drain plug. Giggling, he shoved his pile of paper into the chalk circle and poured the heater oil over it. The demon pulled away from the oil, as if it didn't like it. Derrick awkwardly waved the heater so that oil splashed on the demon's branches and leaves. Then he tossed a lit candle onto the pile of paper.

He smiled as the flames quickly caught and spread, consuming the paper and then spreading to the wood floor, aided by the oil liberally splattered everywhere. The demon grew frantic, circling around the far edge of the chalk line, waving its branches in obvious distress. The breeze lifted a shred of still-burning paper and blew it into the demon's branches. Suddenly the branches were alight, crackling with a ferocity that surprised Derrick. He thought green wood wasn't supposed to burn well. Little black pellets rained out of the branches to bounce and roll across the floor, but Derrick didn't pay them much attention.

The flames grew higher, engulfing the demon. The heat became intense. Suddenly Derrick shook his head. *What the hell was he doing?* Shit! He wasn't an arsonist. Why did he think lighting a fire in an old wooden hotel building was a good idea?

He grabbed his suitcase, skirted the column of flame that now licked across the ceiling, and dashed out the door, yelling, "Fire!"

# Chapter 18

## *Banishment*

Alex strung out the fairy lights in a wide circle around the demonic plants. "I don't know if this string will reach around them all. We might have to do this twice." Two days after Katie's aunt Rachael had visited, Alex and Shel were ready to try to banish the compulsion plants.

Shel laughed. "Not likely. Remember what happened to the lights last time we banished a demon." The lights had been completely fried—bulbs burst and wires smoking. "Make it reach. We've got one string, one chance."

Alex drew the circle more tightly around the patch of demons, wishing they'd thought to go out and buy more fairy lights. The demons' leaves rustled in the dark. Did they know what Alex and Shel were doing?

Did *Alex and Shel* know what they were doing? They'd banished exactly one demon—well, one adult demon and twenty-one of her offspring. They'd worked out that, for the materpoda, they needed to recite the summoning backwards and have lights flickering with exactly the right rhythm in order to open the portal. Computer nerd Shel had found apps to do both.

Yesterday, Rachael had emailed the summoning for *Botane dubia*.

*Leafy splendour, hither come. Though by thy nature deaf and dumb, hear my voice. Heed my call. Into the portal deftly fall. Compelling creature be compelled. Come to me and be bespelled.*

As the descendent of at least one witch, Shel was the one to record the summoning. While anyone could perform a summoning, only one 'born of magic' could reverse it and banish a demon. It was all ridiculously complex as far as Alex was concerned. Why the hell anyone would even *want* to summon a demon was beyond her.

She finished laying out the lights, ending beside Shel. "So have we decided which song to use?" Last time, they'd used the beat of the song 'Call Me Maybe', passed through an app, to flash the lights in the right pattern. This time, they were divided. Alex listened to the trembling leaves of the demons. "I still say the rhythm is slower than 'Ugly Heart'."

"Whether we use 'Ugly Heart' or 'Shout Out to My Ex', the rhythm is the same. I'm not sure the subtle difference in speed will matter," Shel replied. "Besides, I like 'Ugly Heart' better."

"What are you talking about?" asked Katie, who had been quietly standing behind them, watching. She'd insisted on staying up late to witness the banishing. Alex and Shel had agreed to it, giving her the job of turning away anyone who happened by as they worked. Hopefully at this hour, there would be no one else around, but they couldn't count on it.

Shel turned to Katie. "Yesterday, we watched and listened closely to the demons. Even without a breeze, their leaves and branches move. As it turns out, they move in a particular rhythm. They're doing it now. Can you hear it?" They were silent for a few moments while the leaves rustled.

"I guess?" Katie was clearly unconvinced.

Alex continued the explanation. "When Shel and I were

trying to banish the materpoda, the demon kept tapping her feet in a particular rhythm which sounded to me like a song. We worked out that the rhythm the materpoda was tapping out was the one that we needed the lights to flash to for the banishment."

"It's easy to create the right flashing rhythm by using an app that flashes lights to music, so when we listened to the compulsion plants, we tried to match their leaf shaking pattern to a song," explained Shel. "Can you show her, Alex?"

Alex tapped her phone a few times, and the song 'Ugly Heart' by G.R.L. blared tinnily from the speaker, accompanied by flashing fairy lights.

When the song was over, Alex said, "Shel thinks the demons' rhythm matches 'Ugly Heart', but I think it's slower, like 'Shout Out to My Ex' by Little Mix. Here, I'll play that one. Maybe you can decide, Katie." Alex tapped the screen again and 'Shout Out to My Ex' began to play, lights flashing.

Alex watched Katie as she listened, her face dimly lit by the streetlights. After a moment, Katie's eyes widened and she sucked in a breath. "Look!" She pointed at the plants.

The demons had started thrashing wildly in time with the music and flashing lights.

"Ha!" Alex said. "See? What did I say? This is the right rhythm."

Shel sighed. "I suppose."

Alex rubbed her hands together. "Great. Let's do this." She restarted the song with the sound muted, so that the lights flashed silently, then set her phone on the ground and grabbed Shel's arm. After Shel was nearly sucked into the portal they'd opened for the materpoda, Alex wanted to be ready to hold him back when the portal opened this time. She turned to Katie. "Step back, well away from the circle. This might be ... dramatic."

On his own phone, Shel started the backwards recording of the summoning. A thrill of nerves shot through Alex. Were they really doing this again? Did they have it right? Just because this worked for the materpoda didn't mean it would work for a different demon.

The weird lilt of Shel's voice played backwards seemed to be swallowed up by the darkness. Alex rubbed her sweaty palms on her jeans and grasped Shel's arm again as the incantation finished.

A loud crack rent the air, and every bulb on the string of fairy lights exploded in a shower of tiny glass shards. Alex shut her eyes and squeezed Shel's arm. Her eyes flew back open a moment later, when she felt Shel's arm jerk.

Just like last time, the only indication Alex had of the open portal was its effect on Shel. He strained against some invisible pull, his eyes squeezed tightly shut. Ready for it this time, Alex quickly dragged him away from the circle, out of the influence of the portal.

Shel turned and opened his eyes. "It's open," he panted.

"But they're not leaving," Alex said, worry creeping into her stomach. "Why aren't they going through?"

"What the hell is that?" Katie asked.

"Can you see the portal?" Shel's eyes were fixed on a point somewhere within the circle. A point Alex couldn't distinguish from the darkness. It made sense that Katie could see it, since her great-great-grandmother was a witch. Apparently, you had to be 'born of magic', as Gran's book put it, to be able to see a magic portal. Alex felt oddly left out, blind to the portal in front of her.

"You mean that ... rip in the air?" Katie's voice shook. "I thought you guys were crazy. Thought this was all bogus."

Alex nodded. "Yeah. Me too. But Shel, why are they not going through? They should be going through." Fear crept up her spine. The demons should be leaving.

"I don't know. Maybe we have to ... show them the way?" Shel stepped forward.

Alex yanked him back. "No you don't. If anyone's going in there, it'll be me, because I won't get sucked into the portal."

"Huh?" Katie sounded completely confused.

"We'll explain later. That portal's not going to stay open for long." Alex ignored the shaking in her knees and stalked forward, stepping over the still-smoking fairy lights. The demons' branches waved in her direction.

Alex made shooing motions with her hands. "Go on. Get out of here. Go home."

The demons' roots remained firmly planted in the soil.

"Where's the portal, Shel?" Maybe they didn't notice it was open. She could point it out to them.

"To your right. About a metre and a half away." Alex took three steps to her right, and Shel called out, "Stop. Right there. Careful not to fall in."

How could she be careful when she couldn't see the thing at all? "Do you think I *can* fall in if I can't even see or feel it?" She hadn't even considered that possibility. Shit!

"Better to not find out."

Alex waved her hands at where she assumed the portal was. "See? Portal. You can go home. Won't that be nice?"

The demons continued to wave their branches at her, but made no move to enter the portal.

"It's closing!" Shel said, his voice rising. "Alex, get them through now!"

How? "The portal's right in front of me?"

"Yeah. And it's getting smaller."

Alex didn't pause to think. She reached out to the closest demon, grabbed onto a branch and pulled.

Suddenly every demon was thrashing wildly, and the one Alex had grabbed clamped down on her forearm with a claw-like pair of leaves, its other branches lashing at her face and arms.

She cried out and tried to pull away from it, but it kept hold of her wrist. "Let go!" She pried at the leaves around her arm as she leaned away from the slapping branches. Stinging lashes whipped across her face, left, right, left. She shut her eyes and turned her face away from each lash as it sliced her cheeks.

Then the demon let go, sending Alex tumbling backwards onto the pavement of the car park. Her left elbow hit the ground with a jolt of pain, and she swore.

"Alex!"

When she opened her eyes, Shel and Katie hovered over her. "Well, that was a fail." She winced as she sat up.

"Alex. You're bleeding," said Katie, her voice shaking.

"Yeah. No surprise." Alex examined the gashes on her arm, and then gingerly touched her stinging cheeks. Definitely bleeding, but she couldn't really tell the extent of the damage in the dark.

"Venom?" Shel asked. "Do we need to get Thor?" He lifted her arm and squinted, as though he could see traces of venom in the dim light.

"No, I don't think so. It hurts but it doesn't burn like the materpoda bites."

Shel wrapped an arm around Alex, hauling her to her feet. "Come on. Let's get you inside."

Alex let him help her as they followed Katie into the dark and empty pub, even though she didn't actually need help walking. "Sorry I couldn't get them to go through the portal." Worse than the pain was the sick feeling of having failed.

Shel shook his head. "They clearly didn't want to go."

Alex groaned. "What are we going to do?"

Shel gave her a squeeze. "Let's get you cleaned up and bandaged, and then we'll worry about that."

# Chapter 19

## *Another Day, Another ...*

Katie sipped her morning coffee on Wednesday, more bleary-eyed than usual. She'd fired off a long text to Aunt Rachael in the middle of the night, relaying questions from Alex and Shel about the fact the demons hadn't crossed the portal, even though it appeared to be open. She'd gotten no immediate response—she hadn't expected one at two o'clock in the morning—but now her phone buzzed with an incoming message from Rachael..

> **Hmm ... not sure what might have happened. Let me talk to a couple of other witches. I'll get back to you.**

Katie sent a thumbs-up emoji and took another sip of coffee before checking on Alex.

> **You okay this morning?**

**Tired. Otherwise fine**, came Alex's reply.

Well, that was a relief. Katie relayed Aunt Rachael's response and assured Alex she'd let her know if Rachael had any suggestions. She downed the last of her coffee and headed to the Tipsy Teapot to start her workday.

She walked in to find her morning staff all busy hanging garlands, decorating a Christmas tree, and placing Christmas decals on the windows.

"What are you guys doing?" she asked, though it was obvious, and she felt terrible—with all that was going on, she'd completely forgotten that Christmas was only a couple of weeks away.

Jill, wearing a flour-dusted apron, smiled. "Decorating."

"But I didn't buy decorations." Where had they all come from?

Her morning server, Livia, laughed. "My grandad moved to a retirement home in July—his tree and all his decorations were just sitting in Mum and Dad's garage, so I brought them all here. And Neil picked up some coloured lights and tinsel on his way home yesterday."

"Aw, that's so nice of you. I'm sorry I—"

Her barista, Neil, waved her apology away. "You've had so much on your plate. We wanted to surprise you with a little Christmas cheer. Hope you don't mind that we just did it."

Katie's heart swelled. She had the best staff. "It's brilliant! Thank you so much, and let me know how much you spent, Neil, and I'll reimburse you for it. You shouldn't have to be buying stuff for the bar out of your own money."

"Sure, whatever." Neil's tone said he wouldn't be submitting his receipts. Katie made a mental note to order a case of his favourite beer when she talked to her supplier later in the day. She was placing an order for beer in the desperate hope her liquor licence would be restored before Christmas.

Monday's meeting with the liquor licensing board had been mixed. They'd ignored all her data on alcohol consumption. "How do we know you haven't simply made up those numbers?" one of the board members had asked. But they had agreed to a probationary period, in which they would monitor the situation—sending someone out daily to inspect the pub and ensure there was no alcohol on the premises, and to monitor activity in the car park.

"Be aware that you could be forced to shut down if the disruptive behaviour in the car park doesn't stop, whether it's alcohol fuelled or not," the board chairman warned.

Yeah. Katie knew. The worry kept her strung so tight, she couldn't sleep at night. She'd sunk all her money and her heart into the Tipsy Teapot. To lose it would be devastating.

So she agreed to being monitored. A guy from some security company would come out, starting tonight, inspect the building for alcohol, and then hang out in the car park to monitor customer behaviour. The idea of close monitoring made Katie nervous, but it wasn't all day. And if it got her licence back, it'd be worth it. With her staff decorating the place, she passed through into the kitchen, grabbing an apron on her way. She'd scheduled herself in the kitchen this morning—a treat for herself, and a favour for her morning chef, Xavier, who'd gone to a concert last night and wanted the day off, knowing he'd be nursing a hangover today.

In the kitchen, Katie could focus on food, which was her passion, and ignore the problems of business ownership. She surveyed the racks of cooling baked goods Jill had made. They smelled amazing and looked fabulous.

"You've outdone yourself again, Jill," Katie said as Jill returned to the kitchen to finish the morning's prep work.

Jill slid a tray of pork pies into the oven. "I was thinking, Katie."

"Hmm?" Katie retrieved a bag of red peppers from the fridge and began chopping them.

"If you don't get your liquor licence back, there's nothing wrong with running the Tipsy Teapot as a straight cafe."

"Yeah, I thought of that. I know it wouldn't be the end of

the world, but most of our profit comes from the evening crowd, and the alcohol sales are a big part of that. It would mean seriously scaling back." The thought was a stone in Katie's stomach.

"True, and I guess you'd have to change the name."

Katie laughed. "Maybe we could call it the Tea-totaller."

Katie was almost relaxed by the time Michaela arrived to relieve her in the kitchen. She snitched the last chocolate croissant and a cup of tea and headed upstairs to knock back some paperwork and ordering before the dinner crowd arrived.

At about five-thirty, Katie descended to find the dining room quieter than she'd hoped, but not deserted. Quentin, one of the night's runners, was leaning on the kitchen window chatting with the line cook, Lane.

"Are all the salt and pepper shakers full?" Katie asked Quentin, a little miffed he was standing around doing nothing.

"Just checked them," he replied.

"Cutlery wrapped?"

"Done."

"Menus?"

"Molly and I wiped them all down and added the day's specials to them. We set aside two that were damaged."

Damn. It *was* slow. How was she going to keep her staff busy tonight?

"Hey Katie," Lane called through the window. "Since it's quiet tonight, is it okay if I teach Quentin some stuff back here? He's considering culinary school and—"

"Yeah, that sounds great." Katie turned to Quentin. "I thought you were studying accounting."

Quentin shrugged. "Yeah, I am. Accounting's okay, but working here ... well, it was supposed to just be a way to pay the rent, you know. But I really like it. I never considered becoming a chef, but I guess now I want to learn more."

Katie smiled. "Well, Lane is great at what he does. He's the perfect person to teach you. Go on. I'll be out here all evening. I'm sure Molly and I can take care of things."

With a grin, Quentin hurried into the kitchen.

Well, that solved part of Katie's problem. She touched base with Taine and asked him to make a list of mocktail ingredients she should order for the weekend. Then she sidled up to Tui, who was making use of the lull to organise their eclectic collection of teacups by colour.

"If you need me to take the night off, you know, to save on your costs, that's okay," Tui said.

"No way. I guaranteed you certain hours."

"Yeah, but I know you're losing money on nights like this."

Katie raised a hand. "I'm not going to be the type of boss who jerks employees around like that. I want you all to be able to count on your hours and your pay cheques."

"But I'm *volunteering*. As a friend."

Katie was touched, but she knew Tui lived pay cheque to pay cheque because she was putting her younger sister through med school.

"And I'm saying I need you to work your shift. Unless you *want* the night off?"

Tui glanced over Katie's shoulder and smiled. "Oh, not anymore. I intend to get out the popcorn instead and stay right here."

What was she talking about? Katie turned to find Finn

Laird sauntering across the room towards the bar. He smiled at her, and she smiled back. Tui gave her a shove. "I think you've got a customer," she muttered. Then she raised her voice. "Taine, could I get some help in the kitchen for a minute?"

Taine smirked as he passed Katie. Those two were obviously determined to get Katie and Finn together.

Well, maybe tonight would be the night he'd ask her out. Katie focused on Finn. "You know it's only Wednesday, right?"

Finn laughed. "Am I throwing you off, coming in on days that aren't Friday?" He sat down on a stool and leaned towards Katie. They were the only two in the place at the moment. "Pretty quiet today."

Katie bit back a sigh and forced her voice to sound bright. "It'll pick up later. It's still early for the dinner crowd. What can I get you?"

"Still no beer?"

Katie's face must have shown her pain and frustration, because Finn quickly said, "It's fine. I really like the mocktails. I just ... sorry. Any luck on restoring your licence?"

Way to ruin her flirty mood. "We're being monitored for a couple of weeks, so we can prove to them that we're not serving alcohol, or somehow encouraging people to do stupid things in the car park." What would Finn have to say if she told him what the real problem was, and that she was currently consulting with several witches, including her Aunt Rachael, to eradicate the demons that had taken up residence in the car park? She decided not to find out. "What can I get you tonight?"

"How about ginger and lime crush? And, can I see a menu?"

Katie raised her eyebrows. "Two meals in five days? Did

you get kicked out of your flat? Flatmates refusing to do the dishes or something?"

Finn huffed a laugh. "No. Sh—" He cut himself off and hesitated, holding Katie's gaze. "I live alone."

Oh. That sounded like someone who wasn't living alone voluntarily. Divorce? Bad break-up? Katie busied herself fixing his drink. She half wished Tui and Taine would return. She wasn't sure she was up to flirting this evening.

She pulled a slice of lime out and fitted it to the edge of the glass. What the hell. Maybe flirting wasn't on the cards, but perhaps Finn needed someone to talk to. Wasn't that what a good bartender was for? He was often moody when he came in—maybe he was going through a rough time.

She turned and set the drink down in front of him, along with a menu. "Want to talk about it?"

"Talk about what?" Finn asked.

"Why you live alone." Boy, that sounded stupid. "I mean. You know. I live alone, but that's by choice. It just sounded like ..." Maybe she should shut up.

Finn smiled and dropped his eyes to his drink. "Yeah. I don't live alone by choice. It's a pretty recent development."

"Divorce?"

His eyes flew to hers for a moment, then he chuckled. "No. I didn't marry her." He took a sip of his drink. "To be honest, I miss her dogs more than her."

Katie completely failed to hold in her laugh. "Sorry. I'm sorry." She schooled her face into a sombre expression. "That was inappropriate."

Finn's eyes danced. "No. I suppose it's funny, when you think about it. Sarah moved in with me about a year ago with her two chocolate Labs. We were dating at the time, but moving in together was really about the dogs—she couldn't find a flat that allowed pets."

"So you were convenient?" Katie asked.

"I suppose I was. I own a house in Darfield. Big yard for the dogs, plenty of space." He twirled his glass between his hands, his face thoughtful. "I guess she was convenient for me, too. She's a high school maths teacher. Got home before I did every day, and had dinner on the table when I got home." He shrugged. "Sounds horrible and straight out of the 1950s, but it's not like I expected it of her just because she was my girlfriend. It just sort of happened. I'd take the dogs for a long walk every evening while she did her grading or lesson plans or whatever."

Katie nodded. "Convenient."

"Yeah." He lifted the menu without looking at it. "Any suggestions?"

"The ginger tofu with vegetables goes really well with your drink."

"Tofu?" Finn frowned.

"You should try it." Katie smiled, some of her flirtiness returning. "It's my own recipe."

"Well, in that case, bring it on."

Katie sent his order to the kitchen and turned back to Finn. "So, what happened?"

"To my convenient arrangement with Sarah?" Finn grimaced. "Some dude named Trevor. She sprung it on me via text while I was at work. That was the first day I came in here. Didn't want to go home to an empty house."

Ah, so that's why he frowned at his beer that day. "Ouch. He have a bigger yard for the dogs?"

Finn chuckled. "Maybe so." Then he sighed. "I'm really fine with it. I wasn't kidding when I said I miss the dogs more than her. Nothing wrong with her or anything—I really enjoyed her company, and I liked her a lot. I guess it just wasn't the right fit, she and I."

Katie frowned, that little niggle of suspicion still lingering. "Why did you come in here and not go to your uncle's restaurant the day your girlfriend left?"

Finn cocked his head. "How do you know my uncle owns a restaurant?"

Katie felt herself blush. "Um ..."

"Have you been stalking me online?" Finn smiled.

"No." Katie knew Finn didn't believe her denial, so she asked her question again.

Finn laughed. "Uncle Bernard is nosey and talkative. I couldn't face him that day."

At that moment, Tui and Taine returned from the kitchen. Katie stepped back from Finn. "Well, now that I've performed my bartender duty—you know, psychological counselling—I'll leave you to your drink. Your dinner won't be long."

Finn saluted Katie with his glass and gave her a wink.

Tui raised her eyebrows in a question. *He ask you out?*

Katie gave a wee shake of her head. *Not yet.* She wished she'd asked the burning follow-up question she had for Finn—why do you keep coming back here?

# Chapter 20

## *Biocontrol*

Alex and Shel strolled down the footpath, headed to the Tipsy Teapot. They wouldn't normally go out for dinner on a Wednesday night, but they wanted to chat with Katie and support her business until she got her liquor licence back.

"Maybe we should have texted," Shel said. "It's possible she's busy."

Alex shook her head. "Wednesdays have always been slow, and I know she was keeping her schedule open this evening because it's the first day they're being monitored by the licensing board. She wanted to be available to address anything that came up."

They rounded the corner into the car park—Alex wanted to check the compulsion plants, just to make sure they weren't spreading.

A beefy guy in the uniform of some private security company was standing in the car park, right in front of the demons. Their branches were waving at his back as his eyes scanned the car park.

A young couple left the building and headed to their car. The man opened the door of the car for the woman and she stopped for a long kiss before getting in.

The security guy started making kissing noises in their

direction.

"Oh shit," Alex said, pulling Shel along behind her as she hurried forward. "We need to get that security guy away from the compulsion plants before *he's* the one acting drunk in the car park."

She neared the man, who was swaying slightly, as though he was dizzy. How long had he been standing here? Well, he should be highly suggestible. "Excuse me," she said, catching his attention as she and Shel approached. "You look exhausted. There's a nice picnic table over there you could sit at. You can see the whole car park from over there." She pointed towards the table the staff used for their breaks on the other side of the car park. "Why don't you go sit down?"

The man nodded, a bit glassy-eyed. He took a step and staggered a little. Shel swooped in and grabbed him by the arm. "Here, let me help you over there. It's a great place to sit and monitor the car park."

With Shel's help, the man stumbled to the table and flopped heavily onto the bench. "Thanks." He frowned and shook his head.

"I'll ask one of the kitchen staff to bring you a glass of water," Alex said, patting his hand. "Just sit here for a while."

They headed inside and aimed for the bar first. After explaining that the security guard outside was in need of water, they ordered drinks and grabbed a menu.

"Is Katie around this evening?" Alex asked.

"I think she's in the office upstairs," the bartender replied.

"Can you let her know that Alex and Shel are here, and we'd love to chat with her? No rush, though, if she's busy— we're going to have a meal."

When the server brought their drinks, she said, "Katie will be down in a bit."

Alex was just scraping the remnants of gravy off her plate

with her knife when Katie jogged down the steps. "Alex and Shel. Nice to see you. You wanted to chat?"

Alex glanced around the half-full dining area. "Maybe in your office?"

Upstairs, Alex explained to Katie the idea she had for eliminating the demonic plants. "I was thinking, since we can't cut them down or dig them out, and since herbicide was spectacularly ineffective, and banishment didn't work, we could try biocontrol."

"Biocontrol?" Katie frowned.

Alex laughed. She sounded like a nutter, but this might be their only hope. "Gran was really into it," she said. Let Gran take some of the blame for Alex's crazy idea. "It's when you use a predator or disease to control a pest. You know, like how ladybugs eat aphids?"

"Okay. Is there something that eats demonic plants?" Katie's voice was thick with skepticism.

"There's this demon, *Gryllus*." Alex opened the book she'd brought with her. *Formulae for the Summoning of Minor Angels and Daemons* had been her grandmother's book. As it promised, it contained details on how to summon a range of strange creatures. *Gryllus* looked like a humpbacked, oversized cricket.

"A demon." Katie glanced at the illustration in the book and shuddered. "You want to summon another demon?"

Alex nodded. "To eat the plants."

"Are you crazy? What's this monster going to do after it eats the demonic plants?"

Shel leaned forward. "When it's done eating the plants, we'll banish it."

"What makes you think it will work? You tried to banish the plants, and that failed." Katie crossed her arms over her chest.

Alex hadn't expected it would be easy to convince Katie to let them try. "Shel and I spoke to your aunt this morning."

"You talked to Rachael? She never got back to me when I relayed your questions."

"Yeah. I guess she felt she needed to talk to us directly, so she tracked us down online. She had some questions for us, and we ended up with more questions for her." Alex waved a hand. "We really just needed to have a proper discussion."

"Anyway," Shel broke in, "Rachael thought that the reason the banishment failed might have been because we weren't the ones to summon the compulsion plants in the first place."

"Plus," Alex added, "the seedlings might not have entered the portal because they were born here. They might not recognise their own world as home. At least, that's what Rachael thinks."

"How do you know this thing will eat only the compulsion plants? Looks like the thing could mow down anything it wants to."

"According to Rachael, a demon summoned by a witch must perform the task given to it," Alex said.

"And the book says this one, *Gryllus*, is difficult to summon, but easy to control," Shel added.

Katie sighed and took the book. "Let me see what it says." She read the page about *Gryllus*, and then flicked through the book, stopping to read occasionally. Alex waited patiently. To be honest, she wasn't entirely certain this was the best plan, but the alternative was for Shel to learn how to cast a killing spell, and that was terrifying. Only someone 'born of magic' could cast a killing spell, and Shel was the only one, other than Katie, Alex knew who was the descendent of a proper witch. He'd have to cast a new spell for each individual plant, and there were dozens of seedlings in addition to the original four.

And each casting had the chance of backfiring and killing the caster.

Katie frowned. "It says here, *The summoning of spirits shall not be undertaken in jest or without dire need. Significant dangers beset the witch involved in summoning even the most benign of spirits.*" Her eyes scanned further down the page, and she continued to read aloud. "*If a witch neglects to provide a defined task or sufficiently powerful control, any spirit can become a danger to the magic wielder and others.*"

"And so we'll give it a very specific task, and then banish it immediately," Shel said. "This whole thing might only take fifteen minutes—summon it, let it eat the plants, and then banish it."

"We could do it tonight," Alex said.

Katie blew out a breath and closed her eyes. "Is there really no other way to get rid of them?"

"Not that we can come up with. For what it's worth, Rachael agreed with us."

Katie laughed. "I'm seriously beginning to question Rachael's judgement."

Despite the convincing arguments Alex had presented to Katie, the idea of summoning a biocontrol agent for the compulsion plants made her nervous.

She and Shel were going to summon a demon.

On purpose.

She rang Margaret, the only living person she knew who had purposely summoned a demon.

"Would it make you feel better if I was there?" the older

woman asked.

"Yes, please." Alex was thankful Margaret suggested it, because she hated to ask.

As it turned out, Margaret brought Pauline and Ellen with her. Pauline wore her signature gumboots, and Ellen had a straw sun hat jammed onto her head, even though it was midnight.

"I couldn't pass up the opportunity to see this," Ellen said. "I took a nap earlier so I'd be able to stay awake."

Pauline carried a machete. "Just in case." Alex didn't think it would help, if *Gryllus* went amok, but it couldn't hurt.

Shel had recorded the summoning, read aloud from Gran's book, earlier. It was queued up on his phone and ready to play both forward and backwards for the summoning and banishment. They had two new strings of fairy lights, which they strung out around the compulsion plants. They'd use one for the summoning, and if it blew up, they'd plug in the second for the banishment.

They'd even chosen a song for the lights to flash to, purely on speculation. They had nothing to go on to choose a rhythm, but when Shel joked that they should use Weird Al's 'Eat It', nothing else seemed appropriate. They set up Alex's phone to control the music and lights.

They were as ready as they could possibly be. Still, Alex's stomach churned and her palms were sweaty as she stood next to Shel inside the circle of lights.

"Remember, once it's here, you're going to tell the *Gryllus* to eat all the compulsion plants," she said.

"Yep." Shel nodded.

"And you're sure your phobia isn't going to be a problem?" He'd been terrified of the materpoda she'd accidentally summoned earlier in the year.

Shel shook his head. "It's only cen-cen-centipedes I'm

afraid of."

"Aren't you going to create a circle of chalk, or salt, or flour?" Margaret asked. "I'm sure I did that when I summoned Leo."

Alex shook her head. "It doesn't appear to be necessary. The circle with the star in the middle, with precisely placed candles isn't what makes a summoning or banishment work. It's the rhythm of the flashing light."

"Ready?" Shel asked.

"I suppose," Alex replied nervously. She hit the play button, and the lights began to flash. Although she had the volume turned down, the tune spun through her head. How fitting it was that they were summoning a demon to Weird Al.

Shel started the recording of the summoning, and his voice blared out from his phone.

*Gryllus, hopper of the dark*
*Fill the night-time with thy bark.*
*Feeler, wing, leg and claw*
*Hearken when thou hear'st my call.*

A lightning crack shattered the air, and both Alex and Shel took involuntary steps backwards as a leggy creature the size of a large dog materialised in front of them. It had a humped back, like the illustration showed, and its legs were spiked with hairs and spines. Two long antennae on its head lashed like whips. Below the antennae, a pair of mandibles like garden shears snipped at the air.

Before Alex or Shel could say anything, the creature ... *barked*. At least that was the best description Alex could come up with for the sound it made, though it was like no dog she had ever heard.

Shel shook his head. "What? No!"

"Give it the command, Shel," Alex hissed. "Now, before it decides to do something else."

"Um ..." His voice shook. The *Gryllus* barked again and took a jerky step towards them.

"No, she isn't edible!" Shel pulled Alex with him as he took another step backwards.

Was the *Gryllus* talking to Shel? Alex gripped his arm. "Shel! Tell it to eat the plants!"

Shel shook himself. "You, *Gryllus*. Eat the ... eat the demonic plants."

The creature's antennae waved, sweeping around in a circle. The moment one touched one of the compulsion plants, the demon sprang, latching onto the plant with its jaws while the plant thrashed and snapped ineffectively at its hard carapace.

Alex winced, recoiling at the violence of the scene. It was like the compulsion plant was being fed into a chipper. The *Gryllus* snarled and devoured leaves and branches like candy. Bits of compulsion plant littered the ground.

Behind Alex, Pauline swore. "That's one hell of a biological control agent."

"You certain you can banish it?" Margaret asked.

"Look at it go!" exclaimed Ellen. "It's on to the second one."

Alex glanced at Shel. Even in the dim light of the street lamps, he looked pale. She squeezed his arm. "You okay?"

"Maybe?"

"Be ready with the banishment." Alex scanned the ring of fairy lights. It looked like the string of lights had survived the summoning. They still flashed to the silent music.

Margaret sidled up to Alex. "I know I mentioned it before and you said it wasn't necessary for the summoning, but isn't the salt or chalk circle meant to act as some kind of containment for the demon? What's to stop the *Gryllus* from taking off somewhere?"

A frisson of fear shot through Alex. "I don't know—I've never purposely summoned anything before."

Margaret shrugged. "Well, I suppose if you do the banishment quick enough—oh dear."

The *Gryllus* snapped up the last seedling and sprang clear over the motley hedge surrounding the car park to the grassy verge.

"The banishment!" Alex shook Shel's arm. He stood frozen, eyes wide, face pale. His phone slipped from his hand and landed with a crack on the pavement.

Alex swore and dove for the phone. She picked it up and turned it over. Relief flooded her—it was intact. "Shel, your password."

He still stood dumbly beside her.

Heart racing, Alex gripped Shel's chin and forced him to look directly at her. "I need your phone password. We need to play the banishment now."

"B-b-b-but ..."

Alex grabbed his hand and pressed his thumb against the home button. *Please work, please work.* There wasn't time to try all ten of his fingers to see which one he used for fingerprint recognition. The screen lit up, but it was still locked. *Damn it!* She tried the other thumb. Shel watched in a daze as she manipulated his fingers.

"Yes!" The phone unlocked. Alex pressed play on the banishment recording, and Shel's voice, now weirdly distorted by being played backwards, rang out through the darkness.

The blinking fairy lights were incongruously cheery as they all waited breathlessly for the spell to finish. Alex shut her eyes an instant before the crack and flash that told her a portal had opened within their circle of lights.

The crack brought Shel back to his senses. He sucked in an audible breath.

Alex turned to him again. "The portal is open, right?" Shel nodded. "Tell the demon to go back home."

Still pale, Shel raised his voice and called, "*Gryllus*, go home," as though he were talking to a stray dog.

The demon turned towards Shel and barked.

Shel frowned. "What? No, there's not more of them. You've done your job, now go home."

*Bark-bark-bark.*

"That's not what I meant. I meant just these ones." Shel flailed an arm towards the scattered remains of the demonic plants. "You need to go home." His eyes darted towards where Alex assumed the portal hovered. "Go home now!"

"It's closing, isn't it?" Alex asked. Without waiting for an answer, she raced out onto the street, waving her arms, trying to shoo the demon back towards the portal. "Go on. Listen to Shel. Go home!"

*Bark-bark-growl.* The *Gryllus* lunged towards Alex, and she stumbled back, landing on her butt in the middle of the street. It took another leap, over her head, and vanished into the darkness beyond.

# Chapter 21

## *Surprise!*

"Well. That was a fail." Pauline's voice was calm, and perhaps a little amused.

"That was more than a fail!" Katie's knees trembled so violently, she wasn't sure how she remained on her feet. Nothing could have prepared her for the surreal scene she'd just witnessed. "What happened? Why didn't it do what you told it?" She rounded on Shel.

Shel ran his fingers through his hair, clearly as upset as Katie. "It said—"

"It *spoke* to you?" Katie had heard it make sounds, but it certainly hadn't spoken.

Shel nodded, and Margaret stepped in. "The witch who summons a demon can communicate with it. I chat with my Leo all the time. He can be quite personable when he's not being, you know, demonic."

"What did it say?" Alex asked.

"It said its job wasn't finished," replied Shel. "It couldn't go back because its task wasn't complete."

"Does that mean there are still more of those plants out here somewhere?" Ellen asked. She sounded almost excited by the prospect. "Have any of you seen any, apart from the ones in the car park here?"

No one had.

Alex sighed. "Well, we've got to catch it, and we should start looking for it now—the thing is fast."

"Catch it?" Katie felt faint. "How?"

Pauline took charge. "Best if we get it before morning—no one wants to wake to the sight of that thing munching on the petunias. We'll need head torches."

"Anyone have a pet carrier?" Alex asked. "A big one?"

"Or a butterfly net?" asked Shel.

Margaret chuckled. "It'll take more than a butterfly net to catch that thing. But I've got some bird netting I use on my fruit trees. We might be able to use that."

"Oh! What if we set up a snare for it?" suggested Ellen. "You know, like Bear Grylls would do."

"Maybe, but that requires us to lure it into the trap," Pauline pointed out.

"I did that with the materpoda," Alex said. "Maybe it would work with the *Gryllus*."

The conversation swirled around Katie. They all seemed so calm, like ... like they'd done this before. As though summoning strange creatures from other worlds, and having them escape into the neighbourhood, was no big deal. *Far out!* Slowly her terror settled into a mild jitteriness, as though she'd had too much coffee.

They appeared to have made a plan. Margaret hurried home to find her netting. Pauline was off to collect rope. Ellen headed home to cut some bamboo stakes, and Shel was winding up the fairy lights.

"Sorry about this, Katie," Alex said. "It wasn't supposed to go this way. Do you have a bag or something I can use to collect the bits of plant left over? We'll use them as bait."

Katie shook herself out of a daze. "Yes, of course. Come on into the kitchen."

Alex followed as Katie opened the back door and flicked on the lights. "You're welcome to stay here, or go home, Katie. You don't need to join us. It's ..."

Katie opened the cupboard where they kept takeaway bags. "Shocking? Terrifying? Weird and overwhelming?"

Alex laughed. "Yeah. All those things."

"And yet you're not freaking out. None of you are." Katie was only barely holding it together, and the others were making plans.

"Oh, we're freaking out. At least, I am. And I know Shel is." Alex shrugged as Katie handed her a paper bag. "But I guess ..." She smiled. "Well, there's something exciting about it, too. I mean, there are these creatures *from another world*. And they're *real*."

"Real terrifying," Katie corrected.

"Of course! And if you think that *Gryllus* and your *Botane dubia* are scary, you should have seen the materpoda we had to deal with last summer." Alex shook her head, and Katie shuddered at the thought.

"No thanks. Glad I wasn't here then."

"Well, anyway, if you want to head home, we'll deal with this."

Katie considered it. There was some comfort in the idea of going home, locking the door behind her, jumping into bed and pulling the covers up over her head. Forgetting about all of this until morning. But ... Alex was right. There *was* something exciting about it. How often did you get the chance to chase down a giant demonic cricket? "I'm in. Let me find my torch."

Twenty minutes later, the six demon catchers assembled in the car park, along with a large grey cat.

"This is Leo," Margaret said, gesturing to the cat, who sat aloof, like a monarch on a throne—he seemed to look down upon the humans arrayed around him. "He has agreed to help us find the *Gryllus*."

Leo meowed, eyes narrowing at Margaret.

Margaret rolled her eyes. "Yes, technically you're required to do what I say, but I did *ask*, not demand." She leaned towards Katie and whispered, "He was quite keen to come, actually. I think he gets bored sometimes."

"We'll set up the trap in the reserve," Pauline said, waving her machete like a blackboard pointer at Margaret and Ellen. "You know where that big gum tree is?"

Alex nodded. "Shel, Katie and I will locate the demon and start luring it that way." She shook her bag of demonic plant parts. "Text me when the trap is ready. I'll let you know where we are."

"If you haven't found the *Gryllus* by then, we'll help you search," Pauline said.

Margaret turned to Leo. "Go with Alex, Shel and Katie."

Leo meowed again.

"Yes. That was an order. You don't have to stay right with them—just let them know if you find the *Gryllus*."

Another plaintive meow.

Margaret rolled her eyes. "I know they can't understand you. You'll figure it out."

"Fine," Alex said. "Let's go," she said to Leo. He hissed at her, but slunk along behind as they headed out, following the direction the *Gryllus* had headed when it bounded away.

Okay, this was officially the most surreal experience Katie had ever had. She was walking through the dark searching for a giant cricket with a talking cat. Aunt Rachael was going to hear about this. A giggle bubbled up. Who else would she tell? Not one of her friends would believe her.

She brought her thoughts back to the task at hand. Alex and Shel were discussing strategy.

"The *Gryllus* said there were more demonic plants to eat," Shel said. "Where do you think they could be?"

"No idea," replied Alex. "Who would have them in their garden?"

Katie's stomach flipped. "Whoever wanted to sabotage my restaurant. That's who."

Shel frowned. "But who could that be? Everyone loves the Tipsy Teapot."

"Not everyone," Katie admitted. "I've had a few bad reviews."

"What for?" Alex sounded outraged.

"Apparently my beer is overpriced, compared to the old pub."

Shel scoffed. "That's no reason to sabotage the business. Besides, the old pub served nothing but Speights. Of course it was cheaper—it was swill."

Katie snorted a laugh. Her dad loved Speights, but she agreed with Shel.

"This isn't helping us find the *Gryllus*," Alex said.

"Well, I can think of only ... five people who would purposely plant *Botane dubia*," Shel said.

"The garden club members," Alex agreed.

"You don't think *they've* been sabotaging me?" Katie was horrified at the thought. Those women had been so nice to her. Could they have been going behind her back to ruin her business?

"Of course not." Shel waved the suggestion away with a hand. "It's clear they'd never seen the plant before it showed up in your car park."

"And we know they tried to take cuttings and failed," Alex added.

"So who else could it be?" Katie asked, frustrated.

A grey form leapt from the shadows, making Katie jump.

*Meow!* Leo slunk between Katie's legs and then darted off to the left.

"Come on! He's got something." Alex picked up her pace, and Katie and Shel jogged after her.

They followed Leo around the corner and up a shadowy driveway. The cat stopped and hissed. Katie followed his glare to a patch of rank weeds along a fence. The hump of the demon's carapace glinted in the streetlights, and the crunch of its jaws was unmistakable. She flashed her torch over it, and it paused for a moment, mid-chew, before resuming, unconcerned by its audience.

"What's it eating?" Shel whispered.

"Looks like grass," Katie replied.

"Do you think it finished eating the demonic plants already?" Alex asked. She nudged Shel. "Ask it. If it's through with the demonic plants, tell it to follow us."

Shel swallowed audibly. "Hey, *Gryllus*." The demon paused again. "If you've finished eating the demonic plants, you need to follow us."

The demon barked through a mouthful of grass, and Katie looked to Shel for translation.

"It says it hasn't finished."

"But it's eating grass, not demons," Katie whispered.

"Go on. Tell it again," Alex urged.

Shel blew out a breath and drew himself up. "*Gryllus*, you need to come with us now. You're eating grass, not demonic plants. It's time for you to go home."

The giant cricket growled and barked a response. Shel went white.

"What did it say?" Katie asked.

"It claims the grass *is* a demon, therefore its job isn't finished and it can't go home."

Alex slowly crept towards the *Gryllus*, her torch trained on its head.

"What are you doing?" Shel hissed.

Alex didn't answer. Instead, she slipped a hand into the paper bag she carried and drew out a scrap of *Botane dubia*. She held it out towards the cricket, and Katie marvelled at how steady her hand was.

Then the *Gryllus* turned to face Alex and she froze, the leaves in her hand trembling. Not so steady now.

The *Gryllus* barked.

"What did it say?" Alex called back to Shel.

"Um ... fuck off."

Katie struggled not to laugh.

Alex addressed the *Gryllus* directly, waving the leaves at it. "Come on, boy. I've got some lovely *Botane dubia* for you. Come and get it."

*Bark-bark-growl-bark.*

"It says it doesn't want any filthy dead *Botane*," Shel translated.

Alex huffed and shoved the leaves back in the bag. "Fine." She returned to Katie's side.

"What now?" Katie asked.

"Well, we're obviously not going to be able to lure it into a trap if it doesn't want the bait," Alex said.

Shel pulled out his phone. "I'll text Margaret. Maybe they can bring the net here." He tapped out a message.

They stood in silence, waiting for Margaret's reply, watching the *Gryllus* as it continued to much away at grass like some bizarre domestic sheep.

Footsteps sounded on the pavement behind them and

they turned. Who was walking around Rifton at one in the morning? What would they think when they saw the *Gryllus*? Oh boy, this night was about to get even stranger.

From the shadows emerged Margaret, Pauline and Ellen, with Leo leading the way. Ellen had a net slung over her shoulder, Margaret wielded a long stick, and Pauline brandished her machete. They looked like a bad casting of the Three Musketeers.

"That was fast," Shel said. "I only sent that text a minute ago."

Margaret glanced towards the *Gryllus* as she spoke. "Leo came and got us. We were already on our way when your text came in."

Had the cat known the *Gryllus* wouldn't eat the *Botane dubia*? Katie shook her head and focused on the conversation going on around her.

"Let's just toss the net over it," Ellen suggested. "Look, Margaret has threaded the rope through the edge so we can cinch it shut."

Shel shrugged. "Sounds like a plan. It's obviously not afraid of us—Alex walked right up to it."

"Still," Alex said. "We should try to be stealthy—it might not be afraid, but I don't think it's stupid."

Alex and Shel took the net and crept side by side towards the *Gryllus*. The demon continued to munch grass, and for a moment Katie thought it was ignoring them. Then she noticed the antennae—long and whiplike, they drifted lazily through the air. One waved towards Alex and Shel before freezing. It knew exactly where they were.

Three strides away, Alex and Shel stopped and flicked the net in a perfect arc over the *Gryllus*.

Except the demon wasn't there. The net flopped to the ground with a whoosh.

Katie hadn't even seen it move.

Leo growled behind them and they all turned. The *Gryllus* was on the footpath. It barked twice—Katie was certain it was laughing—and then leapt again, vanishing into the darkness.

Leo took off at a run, and everyone followed. They dashed down the street and into someone's garden. Leo barrelled through the yard and, without slowing, vaulted over the back fence.

"Shit!" Shel hissed.

"Come on, we'll go around." Alex doubled back, and everyone followed.

Katie's breath was coming in gasps by the time they rounded the block and caught up with Leo and the *Gryllus*. The giant cricket was once again placidly grazing on grass, this time mowing down a broad swathe of greenery at the side of the footpath. Katie staggered to a halt, along with the puffing members of the garden group. How those elderly ladies kept up, Katie had no idea.

Alex and Shel kept going, net in hand, and flung it over the *Gryllus*. *Bulls eye!* Alex yanked on the rope, drawing the edges together and bundling the demon inside the net.

Everyone drew near as the *Gryllus* growled and thrashed inside the net.

"Hey, calm down," Shel said to the demon. "We're not going to hurt you. We're just sending you home."

"Let's take it to my place," Alex suggested. "We can put it in the materpoda cage and do the banishment from there."

"Um ..." Katie watched the wriggling *Gryllus*. It was easily the size and heft of a Saint Bernard. "How?"

"I'll get my car; we can pop it into the boot," Margaret said. "My place is just round the corner."

While Margaret fetched her car, Pauline turned her torch

onto the grass where the *Gryllus* had been eating. "Huh. Twitch."

"What?" Alex asked.

"It was eating twitch—couch grass. You know what it is?"

"Yeah, Gran always grumbled about the stuff in her vegetable garden. I remember it was bad in the potatoes one year—grew straight through some of the tubers."

Ellen stepped over to examine the spot. "A weed that's virtually impossible to kill and takes over everything if given half a chance. You don't think ..." She trailed off.

Pauline smiled wryly. "It *would* explain its behaviour if it were a demon."

Ellen cackled. *Cackled!* As though discovering that a common weed was a demon was *funny!*

Just then Margaret pulled up in a mustard-coloured station wagon that had to be forty years old. She left the engine idling and jumped out to lift the hatch.

Katie helped Alex and Shel heft the netted *Gryllus* into the back.

"Everyone in," Margaret said as she opened the driver's door. "It'll be tight, but we'll fit."

Thankfully it was a short ride. Katie was squished into the middle of the front, straddling the gear stick. She was wishing she had squeezed into the back until Shel's nervous voice called out, "It's chewing through the net."

"Step on it, Margaret!" Alex yelled.

Katie was jerked backwards as Margaret sped up.

"Hold on." Margaret's face was set in determination, her hands tight on the wheel as they reached an intersection. She was going to turn at this speed? Katie wrapped an arm around the passenger headrest and shut her eyes as the car lurched around the corner with a squeal of tyres.

Another lurching turn, and Alex was barking directions

to Margaret. "Back in, across the grass, beside the house. I'll open the gate to the back garden." She launched herself from the car when Margaret slowed, and swung open the gate.

"It's nearly out!" Shel's voice shook.

The instant Margaret stopped the car, the remaining passengers flew out and slammed the doors shut. Alex tossed a set of keys to Shel. "Go turn the flood lights on in the back. Open the cage."

Shel caught the keys and pounded up the stairs to the front door.

Alex grabbed hold of the hatch, but Katie slapped her hand over it. "Wait! What's the plan?"

"No time to plan. That thing will be out of the net soon. We open the hatch, grab it and run."

With that, Alex lifted the hatch. Katie lunged in with her and hauled on the net.

"Come on, move!"

"Let me pull the hole closed." Katie snagged the ragged edges of the gap the *Gryllus* had chewed. "Okay, go!"

The creature was heavy. They half carried, half dragged it through the gate into the yard. They were mere metres from the big cage in Alex's back yard when a terrible ripping sound came from the net. Suddenly, there was no weight to it and Katie and Alex both stumbled backwards.

Pauline, Ellen and Margaret charged from behind and began shouting and trying to shoo the now free *Gryllus* towards the cage. It barked at them and took a great leap, landing on top of the cage.

"Come down here right now!" Shel shouted at it.

*Bark-growl-bark-bark-bark.*

Shel started, as though he'd been slapped. "Why, you little—"

From the shadows under the shrubbery, a long form

emerged, rippling across the lawn on countless black legs. A scream welled up in Katie's throat as the creature darted up the cage like a bristly black shadow, seized the *Gryllus* in two sickle-shaped jaws, and then retreated to the shadows.

"Oh fuck," said Alex.

# Chapter 22

*Here We Go Again*

Alex's tone wasn't frightened, only disbelieving. "We missed one, Shel. Shel?"

Katie turned away from where the ... centipede? ... had vanished. Shel was sprawled on the ground, unconscious.

Alex sighed. "Oh, Shel." Then she turned away.

"Is he okay?" Katie asked. How could Alex be so nonchalant about Shel collapsing on the ground?

Alex waved a hand. "He will be. He has a phobia of centipedes."

"That was one hell of a centipede." Katie heard the panic in her own voice.

"That was a materpoda," Alex explained calmly. "Remember the creature I said I accidentally summoned a few months ago? Well, it had babies, and it looks like we accidentally left one behind when we banished them."

"That was a baby?" Katie wondered if she was about to faint like Shel.

"Well, maybe more like a teenager now, but yeah, not as big as an adult."

Katie leaned heavily against the house.

"Well, now what?" Margaret asked.

"I think we've got things under control now. Remember,

Shel and I have dealt with materpodas before. A little bait, and we'll have this baby in the cage."

"Do you think it ate the *Gryllus*?" Katie asked.

Alex laughed. "Oh yes. Materpodas are insatiable. Vicious, with poison fangs." As though it were no big deal. Katie wished she could faint like Shel.

"Katie, the fairy lights are in Shel's backpack," said Alex. "Get them out and lay them in a circle around the cage." The confidence in Alex's voice as she took charge gave Katie a little reassurance amid the chaos. "Margaret and Pauline, grab some shovels and other long-handled garden tools from the shed, just in case. Ellen, come inside and make us some tea, will you? I'm going to grab some chicken from the freezer to use as bait. Be right back."

Shel stirred as Katie unzipped his pack, still on his back. "You okay, Shel?"

A groan. "Yeah." Then he swore. "That really was what I thought it was?"

"Alex says it was a materpoda."

Shel blanched. "So, we missed one." His shoulders slumped, then he rallied. "Well, at least we know what to do."

Katie couldn't help but smile. "That's what Alex said. She said I should string the fairy lights around the cage."

Shel nodded and sat up. "Yeah. I'll help."

They laid out the lights, and Shel hauled a few extra chairs to the deck. Margaret and Pauline distributed garden implements, and Ellen came out with a tray full of steaming mugs of tea and a tin of cookies. Alex laid a trail of chicken pieces from where they'd last seen the materpoda, leading into the cage, then tied a rope to the cage door, trailing the end to her seat on the deck.

As they sat down with their tea and cookies, Katie said, "Now what?"

"We wait." Alex flicked the floodlights off and settled into her chair.

Katie was exhausted. She'd started work at seven on Wednesday morning and it was now nearing two in the morning on Thursday. Jill would show up at the Tipsy Teapot in two hours, and Katie had planned on being there to talk about a new idea she had for a scone filled with red bean paste. She shut her eyes for a moment. Even if she left now and went home to bed, the most sleep she'd get would be an hour and a half. And Katie doubted she'd fall asleep, with visions of demonic crickets and centipedes skittering through her brain. She pulled out her phone and sent a text to Jill, putting off their meeting until next week.

She didn't realise she'd dozed off until she started awake. It was still dark. The chair next to her creaked, and tension crackled in the air. She glanced around. Everyone leaned forward in their chairs, and Alex held the end of the rope in her hands as she stared intently into the darkness, from which emanated a wet crunching sound.

"Is that the—"

"Shh," Alex hissed. "Yes."

Katie's stomach tightened. A rustle in the grass, and she saw it—a two-metre-long inky stain against the lawn. It crept steadily forward, antennae scouting the way. It found the piece of chicken Alex had left in front of the cage door and paused for a moment to snatch it up. Then it continued forward. Katie's fists clenched. It was halfway through the door. She willed it forward.

The materpoda suddenly jerked back, as though it had encountered something it didn't like. Alex sucked in a breath and adjusted her grip on the rope.

Then the creature was inside the cage, except for a pair of long legs sticking out behind. Alex slammed the door shut, and the materpoda shot to the other side of the cage in fright, banging against the chain link with a jingle. While the animal ricocheted in panic around the cage, Alex lunged for the door to secure the bolt.

A cheer went up from the spectators on the porch, and then Shel leapt into action. "Let's send this thing home now. I don't want it hanging around here any longer than it has to."

"On it now," Alex said. She plugged in the fairy lights and turned on some song on her phone that made the lights flash. Katie didn't recognise the song from the flashing, but it didn't matter, as long as Alex and Shel knew what they were doing.

Alex nodded to Shel. "Ready?"

"As I'll ever be." He tapped his phone and a strange backwards recording of his voice emanated from the speaker. Katie wanted to ask about the song and the spell. She wanted to know how they'd figured out how to summon and banish demons. But she knew she should keep quiet. Her questions could wait.

The strange incantation ended with a loud crack, and Katie cringed, shutting her eyes. She should have been ready for that. She opened her eyes, blinking away the afterglow swimming green in her vision.

Just like before, there seemed to be a ... rip ... in the air. Like someone had drawn back a curtain just enough to peek through. It sat smack in the middle of the cage, and the materpoda's antennae waved towards it.

"Go through! Go through!" Alex and Shel urged the animal on, but it remained still.

No, its legs were moving, readjusting their grip on the ground, as though it was in danger of being sucked into the portal. It was actively *resisting* going through.

Katie stood and banged on the side of the cage to try to scare the creature in. This close, she felt the pull of the portal herself. It was disconcerting, and she was thankful there was chain link between her and the greedy rip in the air.

"Why isn't it going?" she asked Alex and Shel.

"No idea," Alex responded.

Shel picked up a stick and poked it through the cage, nudging the materpoda. It clicked angrily at him and shuffled marginally closer to the portal, but didn't go in.

"I'm going in there," Alex said.

"What? No!" Shel cried.

"Someone's got to, and you sure as hell aren't. You'll get sucked in. Tell me where the portal is. I'll fling it in." Her voice shook.

"Alex, surely there's another way." Katie didn't like the feel of the portal tugging on her, nor did she like the look of the materpoda. And Alex had said they were venomous. What was she thinking?

Alex ignored both Katie and Shel. She slid back the bolt, slipped inside and pulled the door shut, slamming the bolt home again.

"Alex, don't!"

"Shel, tell me where the portal is. I'm doing this."

Shel swore. "It's in the centre of the cage. About fifty centimetres left of the mater—*what*?"

A sleek grey cat leapt lightly out of the rip in the air. *Leo?* But he'd been on Margaret's lap just moments before. Katie glanced back and, sure enough, Leo sat at attention watching the action like everyone else. Katie turned back to the cage.

Alex's jaw dropped open. "Thunder?"

*Meow.* The cat arched his back and hissed at the materpoda. The materpoda responded by lunging at the cat.

"No!" Alex leapt towards the materpoda, but she wasn't fast enough to save Thunder.

But the cat apparently knew what he was doing. He

pressed himself against the ground, and the materpoda, focused on racing towards the cat, was sucked with a pop into the portal just as it snapped closed.

Alex fell to the ground beside the cat. "Thunder, you rascal!"

Leo padded across the deck and circled around to the cage door as Alex and Thunder exited. He and Thunder greeted one another with hisses that Katie thought would turn into a full-blown cat fight. But a moment later, Leo batted Thunder on the head with a gentle paw, and meowed something to the other cat.

Thunder looked directly at Katie and met her gaze, as though he was assessing her. Then he padded to her feet, sniffed, reared up on his hind feet and placed his paws on her knees.

*Well, you'll do I suppose.* The sandpaper-like voice rumbled through Katie's mind.

"Um ... guys? Did this cat just say something?"

*What kind of pathetic witch are you?* He dropped back to all fours and turned away. *Leo, you said she was a witch.*

Leo meowed, and Margaret laughed. "Thunder has chosen you, Katie. He's your familiar now."

"Wait a minute," Alex said. "I thought you were Gran's cat, which would mean you're mine."

*Tell Alex I was never Alice's. The witch who summoned me is long dead. I lived in the pub for a long time. I guarded Room Four. At least until Allison and Mark Young bought the place. She claimed to be allergic to cats. Humph. Served them right the place burnt down.*

Katie relayed what Thunder said. The women from the garden group hung on every word—clearly they knew more about the history of this cat than she did. Alex shrugged and shook her head.

Katie rubbed her face. "You all are going to explain everything to me as soon as I've had some sleep and can take it in." Then she turned to Thunder. "And I am *not* a witch, no matter what you say."

*Ha! That's what you think. I can smell the magic on you.*

Katie surreptitiously sniffed her shirt. God she was tired! Could this night get any weirder?

"Well, I think we're done here," Pauline said cheerfully. She picked up her machete from the ground and added, wistfully, "I didn't even get to use this."

"Maybe next time," said Ellen, patting Pauline on the arm.

"*Botane dubia* gone, *Gryllus* gone, materpoda gone," Alex added. "A busy night's work. Thanks everyone."

"Yes, thank you all," Katie said. "I definitely couldn't have done this myself." Hopefully, this would be the end of her troubles with 'drunks' at the Tipsy Teapot.

"Come on Ellen and Pauline," said Margaret with a yawn. "I'll drive you home. And Katie, if you need any advice dealing with Thunder, don't hesitate to ask me. There's an adjustment period, and demonic cats are ... well, they're cats, so they can be terribly rude at times."

"Um ... thanks." Katie was reeling, and all she wanted to do was go to bed. She glanced around. Thunder was nowhere to be seen. Maybe he'd decided she wasn't worth the bother after all.

The older women left, and Alex handed Katie the bag of *Botane dubia* bits. "Show these to Thunder later. He may know more about them. Hopefully it won't matter anymore, but just in case, it would be good to learn as much as we can."

"Thanks." Katie took the bag. "I'm sorry I didn't believe you when you first talked about these demons and stuff."

Alex waved the apology away. "Shel and I didn't believe it either. It's ..."

"Hard to take in."

Alex smiled. "Especially when you're exhausted. Go home. Get some sleep."

"Don't expect me for our morning walk."

"Yeah, me either. I'll be lucky to roll out of bed in time to get to work." Alex and Shel both hugged Katie, then went inside. Katie smiled. Those two. Alex danced around the question whenever Katie asked about them, but it was clear Shel had no intention of going home tonight.

Not that there was much night left anyway. Katie hurried home, eager to put the evening behind her.

# Chapter 23

## *Christmas Eve*

Christmas snuck up on Katie. The weeks after what she came to call Banishment Night were full of adjustment. The morning after, she'd arrived in her office an hour later than usual to find Thunder curled up on her desk chair. He opened one eye and glared at her.

"How did you get in here?"

*Piss off. I'm tired. Portal lag sucks.* He closed his eyes again.

So it hadn't been the figment of an overtired brain last night. This 'cat' could talk.

"Are you really a demon?"

He didn't bother opening his eyes. *Of course I'm a bloody demon. What did you think I was, a house cat?*

Well, yes, but she knew not to voice that thought. She shook her head.

"You will explain this all later."

*Only if you shut up and let me sleep.*

Katie suppressed a giggle, picked her laptop off the desk, and did her morning's work from the armchair in the office, computer perched on a stool in front of her. Her first order of business was to text Aunt Rachael.

**We got rid of the Botane dubia last night. You will never believe what happened. Call me.**

When her staff asked about the cat, she told them he'd just shown up and made himself at home. It was the truth, if not the whole truth.

Once Thunder was better rested, he was a little less rude. He explained that he'd been summoned by pub owner Mary Saunders in 1918.

"Wait. Was that Shel's great-great-grandmother?" Didn't he say his relative had owned the pub in the early 1900s?

It was, but Thunder had stayed with the pub, rather than with Mary's family.

"But why the pub?"

*Rifton is an unusual place. The barrier separating worlds is weak here. And the very weakest point is in Room Four of the Rifton Pub.*

"In my storeroom."

*Yes. During my tenure at the pub, witches regularly came to perform summonings in Room Four.*

"Did the pub owners know?"

*Mary did. None of the others, though. Some might have suspected—weird things happened in Room Four. I did my best to prevent disaster, but I couldn't prevent everything.*

"And why would a demon care about other demons overrunning Rifton?" This was what confused Katie. What *were* demons anyway? Margaret adored her familiar, Leo. Alex's cat, Thor, was apparently good at healing wounds. The materpoda, *Gryllus*, and demonic plants were weird and terrifying, but they hadn't struck her as *evil*, like demons were supposed to be.

*What do you think would happen if the general public found out there were places where you could cross into another world?*

Ah. Now she understood. "You're afraid that *your* world will be overrun by people. So you stayed here as a ... a gatekeeper?"

*Something like that.*

"You didn't want to go home? Could you have gone home?"

*Once Mary died, I was free to do whatever I liked. I considered going back. I could have used a portal opened by a witch in Room Four—it happened often enough.* The cat seemed to shrug. *But then who would guard Room Four?*

"But you came out of that portal the other night—the one Shel opened. So you must have eventually gone home."

*I did. When Alex and Shel banished the materpodas, two of the babies were nearly stuck on this side of the portal. I managed to drag one across before the portal shut.*

"And then you were stuck on the other side."

Another shrug. *The pub had burnt. No one was using Room Four. It was good to visit home for a while.*

"Why did you come back?"

*Boredom. Besides, I really like tuna. We don't have that in our world.*

Katie made a mental note to pick up some tuna.

The Saturday after Banishment Night, the garden group arrived at the Tipsy Teapot for morning tea. By now, Katie's staff knew their drink orders by heart, and the women had only to sit down and their coffees and teas would be brought to them. Most also had their favourite sweets, and Sharon always had the carrot cake.

No matter what Katie was doing, she made sure to check in with the women before they left. Today when she arrived at their table, Jane immediately said, "I'm so sorry Sharon and I couldn't come help the other day with ... you know."

"It's okay. We managed, and I'm not sure having more people would have helped," Katie replied.

"Mostly we're sorry because we would have loved to be there," Sharon clarified. "It's not every day you get to see" — she glanced around at the busy room— "those things."

"Truth. Thank God for that!" Katie laughed. She cocked an expectant brow at Sharon. "Today's verdict?" This latest version was simpler than some others she'd tried, with cream for a smooth texture and lemon zest to give it more zing.

Sharon sighed, and Katie couldn't help feeling a pang of disappointment. What would it be this time? Too fluffy? Too zingy? Maybe she should have used ginger instead of lemon zest.

"It was the most divine thing I have ever eaten. That frosting was perfect!"

"Really?" Katie laughed incredulously. "I thought I'd never hear you say that." Her sense of accomplishment was way out of proportion with the task, but it wasn't every day you produced the perfect slice of carrot cake. Except from now on, she would. Every day.

Katie got her liquor licence back five days before Christmas. The place was packed on Christmas Eve. Every table reserved in advance, and the bar crowded with drop-ins.

Katie was helping Taine at the bar when Finn Laird arrived. He smiled at her as he claimed the only vacant stool.

"Looks like you're back in business."

Katie smiled. "Yes. And not a moment too soon. Beer?"

"Yes please. The usual."

"Dinner?"

"Of course."

Katie handed him the menu. She moved down the bar, sidling around Taine mixing a mocktail—they were still popular—and pulled Finn's beer. As the glass filled, she glanced at another customer, who had just finished his meal. "Dessert?" she asked.

"Oh sure, why not?" He ordered a slice of green tea cheesecake and a coffee.

When she brought Finn his beer, he was looking around. "The place looks great. Very festive." He glanced up over the bar. "Is that mistletoe? I thought it had white flowers."

Katie's gaze rose to the bunch of large red flowers and spiked leaves she'd hung over the bar. The blooms were remarkably resistant to wilt—it had been weeks and they still looked fresh and smelled sweet. "It's not mistletoe. The flowers are pretty, aren't they?"

It had been a risk, keeping them, hanging them over the bar. It had been Thunder's idea, and at first Katie had wanted nothing to do with it. But apparently there were ways of limiting one's own susceptibility to the blooms, and even directing their effects. Business had been excellent since she'd hung them. She encouraged her staff to always offer sides and dessert. The tip jar had to be emptied several times a night.

Finn nodded. "Very Christmassy."

With Finn smiling at her, Katie had another idea. Was it unethical? Probably not more so than using the flowers to increase sales. She wiped the bar with her cloth, mopping up a non-existent spill. "Gotta celebrate the season that brings everyone out to eat. It's like the dating season." Was that too blatant? Not direct enough?

Finn nodded and sipped his beer. "Yeah, ah ... speaking of dates. I know you work a zillion hours a week, but do you want to go out sometime?"

A jolt of triumph shot through Katie. Finally! She glanced up at the flowers hanging over the bar. She still didn't know how those demons ended up in her car park, but in retrospect, it had turned out well.

When the night finally ended and all the customers were safely bundled out the door, Katie sauntered up to Tui. "You owe me ten bucks."

Tui looked up from the register where she was counting cash. "You said we could eat what we wanted on our break."

Katie laughed. "Not for the pie you ate. Finn asked me out this evening."

Tui squealed and hugged Katie.

After locking up that evening, Katie was surprised to see someone still in the car park. They were bent over by the edge of the pavement. Were they okay? As she neared, they straightened and turned, the head torch they wore shining in Katie's face.

"Margaret! What are you doing here?"

Margaret blushed. "I was ... well, I was cleaning up all the *Botane dubia* seeds. Leo warned me we should collect them so they don't sprout. Otherwise we'll be back to where we started."

"Oh!" Katie hadn't even thought about that. "How can you possibly find all the seeds in the dark?" And why was she doing it at night in the first place?

"Leo is helping—seems he can sniff them out."

Why hadn't Thunder warned her about this? She could have cleaned up these seeds weeks ago.

Just then, Leo emerged from the shadows. Margaret bent down and he dropped a small black pellet into her hand.

"May I see that?" Katie asked, holding out her hand.

The pellet was pea-sized and reminded her of a curled-up slater. "I've seen these before! I swept up a bunch of them from Room Four before the renovators came. I ... I tossed them out under the hedge on the edge of the car park." Realisation dawned.

No one had been trying to sabotage her.

She thought back to the scene in Room Four the first time she saw it. Chalk circle on the floor, melted wax, a perfect circle of scorching. Someone had summoned a demon. *Botane dubia*? But then why the fire? She shook her head. She'd probably never know.

She tipped the seed back into Margaret's hand. The woman carefully dropped it into an envelope labelled *Botane dubia*.

"Margaret. You're not saving those, are you?"

The woman shrugged. "You never know when they'll come in handy."

"Margaret!"

"Relax, Katie." Margaret laid a hand on Katie's arm. "I know what they are. I'm not planting them in my flower garden. Leo felt, and I agreed, that it was better if I held onto them rather than risking them being misused."

"You should throw them out!"

"Like you did?" Margaret's eyebrows rose, and Katie deflated. She was right. "Katie, we don't know how to destroy them. But we can be pretty sure they won't germinate without the right conditions. The safest place for them is in a dry, dark cupboard."

Katie hoped Margaret was right. She left the woman to her seed collecting, vowing to ask Thunder about it in the morning.

The night was warm, and this close to the summer solstice, there was still a faint blush of light in the western sky, even this late at night. Katie smiled as she walked home. Hard to believe that only seven months ago, she was surveying that burnt-out pub for the first time and wondering what the hell Aunt Rachael had gotten her into. She *still* wondered what Rachael had gotten her into, but she was pretty sure it would be interesting, whatever came next.

# Historical Note

The historical interludes in *Demonic Summoning for the*
*Modern Gardener* trace the history of the fictional Rifton
Pub, but are based on the real history of Aotearoa New
Zealand's pubs and taverns, and the country's sometimes
uneasy relationship with alcohol.

European settlers no doubt brought alcohol to Aotearoa
on the first ships to land on its shores. Through the mid-1800s
each province had its own laws around the sale and
consumption of alcohol. In 1881, the Licensing Act
consolidated liquor laws under a national set of rules. This
was the first time New Zealand had a drinking age and rules
about liquor shops' opening hours.

The Licensing Act established a drinking age of 16 for
drinking in pubs. Children of any age could still purchase
alcohol to take home. It also banned the sale of alcohol on
Sundays, Christmas Day and Good Friday.

But the Licensing Act didn't just address who could buy
alcohol and when, it set strict limits on the types of
establishments that could serve alcohol. Pubs couldn't have
concerts, theatrical performances or billiards. Additionally,
any establishment selling alcohol had to provide at least six
rooms of accommodation and offer meals. Thus, many of
New Zealand's old, small-town pubs are called hotels, and
have a few rooms above or behind a restaurant. (It's an

experience to stay in one of these old hotels, with their communal bathrooms, creaky wooden floors, and dated decor and furnishings.)

During the late 1800s and early 1900s, a flurry of legislation raised the drinking age to 21, banned women from owning or working in pubs unless they were family of the owner, and restricted or banned alcohol sales to Māori.

The temperance movement became active in New Zealand during the late 1800s. From 1893, local districts held referendums every three years in which people could vote to restrict the number of licensed establishments in their district, or ban the sale of alcohol entirely. Between 1894 and 1906, 12 districts voted to ban liquor sales entirely.

The Women's Christian Temperance Union and the New Zealand Alliance were formed in 1885 and 1886, respectively, to campaign for national prohibition. Prohibition became a hotly debated and divisive topic.

In the first decade of the 1900s, prohibitionists pushed for national referendums on liquor licensing to be held in conjunction with every general election, hoping to ban alcohol nationwide. The first such referendum was held in 1911, and 56% of voters chose prohibition—4% shy of the 60% threshold required to trigger national prohibition. Subsequent referendums also narrowly failed to trigger prohibition, even when the threshold was reduced to 50% in 1918.

World War I brought further restrictions to the sale of alcohol. In order to preserve resources for the war effort and limit alcohol consumption, bars were forced to close at 6 pm. Originally intended as a war effort, the six o'clock closing time was not changed until 1967.

The efficacy of the six o'clock closing time was limited. Instead of leading to a reduction in alcohol consumption, it led to what was known as the 'six o'clock swill'—an hour of binge drinking. Responding to the six o'clock swill, some bars had no seating and no food, catering to men who guzzled their beer standing up in the hour after work.

The failure of prohibition in America and the onset of the Great Depression saw the support for prohibition in New Zealand falter. By 1935, the national referendum registered only 29% support for prohibition.

It wasn't until the 1950s that liquor laws began to be relaxed. In 1952, the ban on women owning pubs was lifted. The Sale of Liquor Act 1962 allowed for a few restaurants to be licensed, lifted the ban on women working at pubs and eliminated the requirement that pubs provide accommodation, although a large tax was imposed upon pubs without accommodation. In 1967, pub closing times were extended to 10 pm and the ban on entertainment in pubs was lifted. In 1969, the drinking age was lowered to 20.

It wasn't until 1989 that the tax on pubs without accommodation was lifted. At this time, the responsibility for setting pub closing times was handed to local governments. Regular national licensing referendums were stopped, after 76 years, as support for prohibition had never come close to 50% since 1919. At this time, there were still four local districts that were dry based on local referendums, but by 1999, all had voted to go 'wet'.

In 1999, the drinking age was lowered to 18, where it remains today. Today, pubs are required to be closed between 4 am and 8 am, and local governments can further restrict pub opening times.

# Katie's Carrot Cake

Ingredients:
- 4 large eggs
- 1 cup vegetable oil
- 2 tsp vanilla
- 1 cup brown sugar
- 2 cups wholemeal (whole wheat) flour
- 2 tsp baking soda
- 1 ½ tsp baking powder
- 1 tsp salt
- 1 Tbsp cinnamon
- ½ tsp nutmeg
- 2 ½ cups grated carrots
- 1 cup chopped walnuts
- 1 cup raisins
- ½ cup crystallised ginger, finely chopped

Preheat the oven to 180°C (350°F).

Grease and line with parchment, two 23 cm (9-inch) round cake tins, or one 23 x 33 cm (9 x 13-inch) cake tin.

Beat the eggs in a large mixing bowl until frothy. Add the oil while the mixer is running. Then add the vanilla and sugar. Continue to beat until the mixture is thick and foamy.

Combine the flour, baking soda, baking powder, salt and spices in a medium bowl. Add the flour mixture to the egg mixture and mix until smooth. Stir in the carrots, nuts, raisins and ginger.

Pour the batter into the prepared pan(s). Bake for 35 to 40

minutes if using two 23 cm tins, or 45 to 50 minutes if using one 23 x 33 cm tin, until a cake tester inserted into the middle comes out clean. Allow the cake to cool 5 minutes in the pan before turning it out and cooling completely on a wire rack.

Frosting:
   170 g cream cheese (cold)
   ¾ cup icing (confectioner's) sugar
   1 ½ tsp vanilla
   1 cup heavy cream (cold)
   Grated zest of 1 lemon

Using an electric mixer, beat the cream cheese until creamy. Add sugar and vanilla and beat until smooth (at least 2 minutes). Pour the cream in slowly while continuing to beat at low speed. Turn the mixer to high speed and beat until the mixture forms stiff peaks (1–2 minutes).

# Acknowledgements

Every book is a joint effort. Huge thanks to all my early readers for *Demonic Summoning for the Modern Gardener*: Ian, Stefanie, Rachel, Matthew, and Laura. Your critical eyes and fabulous insight were invaluable!

And speaking of critical eyes, thanks goes out to my editor, Belinda, who always saves me from embarrassing mistakes. This time, among other mistakes, her eagle eyes caught the fact that I gave a character in this book the same name as the chicken in the last book. Now that I think of it, maybe I should have run with it. Perhaps Loretta didn't actually die, but was turned into a chicken ...

Thanks also to cover designer, Jenn, who once again came up with a delightful cover that captures the lighthearted craziness that is Rifton.

And special thanks to all my readers, who have come along for this ride. Until next time, I'll see you at the Tipsy Teapot!

# About the Author

Robinne is an entomologist and educator by training, but she has never been able to control her writing habit. She writes fantasy, science fiction, and non-fiction for children and adults.

Robinne tries to include adventure in her stories, and believes adventures are the key to writing. The list of her own adventures is long, and includes teaching with a live two-metre-long Burmese python, living in a mud house in rural Panama, and delivering a pair of goat kids in the middle of a dinner party.

Robinne lives in small-town New Zealand, in a place a bit like Rifton, but without the giant centipedes and biting plants (she is, however, convinced that the magpies are demons, and she's suspicious of one of the neighbourhood cats).

Visit her online at: https://robinneweiss.com, Facebook: AuthorRobinneWeiss, Instagram: @robinneweiss.

# Other Titles by Robinne Weiss

**Cosy Urban Fantasy for Adults**
*Demonic Summoning for the Modern Woman*
*Squelched*

**Epic Fantasy for Young Adults**
*Fatecarver*
*Fatewalker*
*Fatemaker*

**Fantasy for ages 8-13**
*The Dragon Slayer's Son*
*The Dragon Slayer's Daughter*
*The Dragon Defence League*
*Dragon Homecoming*
*Dragons of Aotearoa New Zealand*
*The Ipswich Witch*
*A Glint of Exoskeleton*

**Poetry**
*Pandemic Poetry: Across the Fence*

**Non-Fiction**
*Backyard Bugwatcher*
*Insects in the Classroom*

www.ingramcontent.com/pod-product-compliance
Lightning Source LLC
Chambersburg PA
CBHW050421260626
47156CB00003B/1102